Jennifer McMurrain

Winter
Song

LilyBear House

Winter Song
By Jennifer McMurrain

©2013 by Jennifer McMurrain

Cover Design: Brandy Walker
www.sistersparrowgraphicdesigns.com
Interior Design: Jennifer McMurrain
www.lilybearhouse.com

Published by LilyBear House, LLC
www.lilybearhouse.com

ISBN: 978-0615854472

Also available in eBook publication

PRINTED IN THE UNITED STATES OF AMERICA

Dedication

To my loving husband, Mike. Thank you for all your love, support and friendship. You are the definition of true love.

Prologue

Cooper Davis felt like he'd been smacked by a Mack truck and dragged forty miles. Eight hours; he had eight hours until he had to go on deck. Signing up to be a greenhorn on a fishing vessel to catch cod was a mistake. He knew that, but it was a mistake that would help make his dream of owning a bed and breakfast with his girl, Sage, a reality.

He pictured her as he drifted off. Her face made the pain bearable. Every ache was soothed by her smile. He heard her singing, as she did every morning as she made breakfast. She was a natural morning person, forced to be a night owl to keep her job. But not for much longer, soon she'd make her own hours, and he was going to make that happen.

Sage's cheery voice was soon interrupted by a ringing. It was faint at first but grew louder. Then it was ear-splitting. Cooper bolted up, quickly taking in his surroundings. He was still in his bunk on the *Fancy Nancy* cod boat, Sage a thousand miles away.

"Oh my God. Oh my God. Oh my God," came a chant from the floor. It was Gavin Hart, Cooper's bunkmate and fellow greenhorn.

Cooper hopped out of his bunk and grabbed the survival suits. "It's okay, kid. Just put on your suit. Probably another drill."

But Cooper knew it wasn't another drill, His heart thudded against his chest so violently, he was afraid it would explode.

Taking a deep breath, he peeked his head into the galley. Smoke hazed throughout the cabin as Captain Mullis ran through the galley to get back to the wheelhouse. "Put on your suit, Davis, and then get up on deck and get the life raft ready. We're gonna need it."

"Yes, sir," Cooper nodded and grabbed for his suit.

"There's a hole," Gavin whimpered. "I caught my suit on that nail we're always complaining about, and now there's a hole in my Gumby suit." He looked at Cooper with tears in his eyes. "My mother begged me to stay home. Said I'd die out here. She's right. I'm going to die, aren't I, Davis? I'm never going to see my mother again or Suzie. The whole reason I came on this stupid boat was for Suzie. I want to marry her."

Cooper rolled his eyes. "No one's going to die today." He threw his suit at Gavin. "Put mine on."

Gavin shook his head. "I can't. I can't move."

"Yes you can," said Cooper, helping Gavin slip his feet into the full suit. He pulled the kid up, shoved his hands into the arms, pulled the hood up and zipped the suit as Gavin started to cry.

Cooper grabbed his chin. "You are not gonna die, Hart. Listen up. You're going up on deck and get that life boat ready. Then you're going to get in the damn boat, and you're going to live. The minute you get on land, you hug your Momma and kiss that girl. You hear me?"

Gavin nodded as Cooper pushed him out the door. "I expect to be in the lifeboat as soon as I get my suit on. I'm counting on you, Hart."

The kid gave Cooper one more determined nod before running toward the stairs. Cooper turned and reached for the holey survival suit. With one foot in the suit, the boat listed to port side, causing Cooper to tumble. His mind raced as the boat didn't right itself. It was going down.

Ditching the suit, he struggled to make his way out of the bunk. Captain Mullis lay near the stairs. Water filled the galley as Cooper made his way to the Captain, who was already in his survival suit.

"Captain Mullis wake up!" yelled Cooper.

The captain mumbled, and Cooper could smell the unmistakable scent of whiskey. Captain Mullis was drunk.

"You stupid son-of-a . . . -- what have done?" yelled Cooper.

The cold water felt like tiny shards of glass stabbing Cooper's socked feet as he pulled the captain up the fun house stairs. Defying gravity, he made it to the top just in time to see two more deck hands crawl out of the engine room, smoke billowing out from behind them. Neither had on their Gumby suits.

The men pulled the captain the rest of the way out of the staircase, inflated his life vest, and threw him over the side of the boat and into the frigid waters near the lifeboat.

The boat groaned as it tilted even more, threatening to completely capsize. The men looked at each other, terror on every brow.

"We have to swim for the life boat," said Cooper.

"Are you crazy?" said one of the men. "We'll die of hypothermia. Its better we stay on the boat. The Coast Guard is coming. We'll be safe here."

An explosion from the engine room rocked the ship again, causing the men to stumble. Cooper fell towards the water, grabbing at anything in his path to hold on, but it was no use. He hit the water, the cold causing him to lose his breath instantly.

He tried to remain calm, tried to remember where the surface was. His fingers instantly went numb making it hard to swim, but he reached toward the light as hard as he could breaking the surface just in time to see the boat sinking beneath the waves. The two deckhands were still clinging to the fragmented ship, trying to stay out of the water.

He tried to yell at them to get away from the boat, that the suction would take them down too, but he lacked the air and strength to get his message across. He couldn't help them now, he had to find the life boat. He had to make sure Gavin was okay.

Twirling in a circle, he finally spotted the bright red boat. It was a good hundred yards away from him. He could just make out the Hart kid pulling Captain Mullis into the raft. "Good," he thought, "the kid made it to the raft."

He turned his focus on Sage. He had to get back to her. Mustering all the strength he had left, he swam toward the boat. "I must get back to Sage," were his final words before everything went dark.

Sage McKennan stared into the fireplace and shivered. Cooper knew the one-bedroom house he shared with her was warm enough. It was an internal chill that raced through her body. It happened every time they fought, and this night was no exception.

"Come, sit by me," said Cooper, patting the couch cushion beside him. Sage didn't move.

Cooper sighed and bit his lower lip. "Okay, you were right. I shouldn't have gone. I just thought I could earn us some money for the bed and breakfast. I don't want you to have to work graveyard at the hotel for the rest of your life. You deserve better."

Sage moved from the fire to the window. The snow was coming down hard during this rare April blizzard. The lights blinked. Sage gave a worried glance at the lamp. Cooper walked up behind her.

"Don't worry, baby. The storm will blow over soon enough," he whispered gently. "Just another Wyoming spring. Nothing to worry about."

Sage turned away and rushed to the china cabinet, gathering candles from a top drawer.

Cooper chuckled. "I know. I know. If you light all the candles now, the lights won't go out. If you wait and don't light them, the lights will go off, and you'll be scrambling around in the dark." He smirked. "Of course, you know how I like to scramble in the dark."

Sage set the candles around the small den and began lighting them.

"Come on, Sage!" Cooper groaned. "How long are you going to keep giving me the silent treatment? I've been through hell. I don't even know if anyone else made it off the boat. The only thing I could think about was getting to you. Speak to me! Tell me you love me! Let me hold you. Why are you being so stubborn?"

Sage looked up as headlights fell through the window.

"Who in the world is that?" asked Cooper.

Sage hurried to the back door, opening it in time to let the Deputy in out of the snow. He stomped his boots off before stepping out of the mudroom.

"Deputy Park," said Cooper, "I bet you're here to ask me about the accident. Sage, please get the man some coffee."

"Please sit down, Richard," said Sage, gesturing to the small kitchen table. She hurried to get the coffee pot that warmed on the stove. "I'm sure you're chilled to the bone. I hate nights like this."

Richard sat, holding his hat in his hands.

Cooper leaned on the doorjamb. "I really don't remember much. You should've called. I would've saved you the trip. All I know is the alarm went off, and I grabbed my survival suit. This kid by the name of Gavin Hart was my bunkmate, couldn't have been more than eighteen. He did the same. Then he started freaking out 'cause his suit had a hole in the foot. So I traded with him. Next thing I know, I'm swimming in the Bering Sea."

Sage handed Richard a large cup of steaming coffee. "Well?" she asked.

Richard placed the coffee on the table untouched, grabbed Sage's hand, and shook his head. "It's not good, Sage. You better sit down."

Sage sank into a chair.

Richard rubbed his thumbs over the back of her hand and cleared his throat. "They found one lifeboat. Captain Mullis and some kid named Gavin Hart were the only ones in there."

"Oh, good!" Cooper gave a sigh of relief. "Glad the kid made it out."

Sage took in a deep breath. "What about...?" A loud sob finished her sentence as Richard shook his head slowly.

"You mean he's dead?" Sage bolted out of the chair. "Cooper's dead?"

"What's wrong with you, Sage? I'm right here." Cooper closed the distance between them. He reached out to hug her but caught only air as his hands passed through her body. "What the...?"

Sage shivered.

"Do you have someone I can call?" asked Richard.

"She doesn't need to call anyone. I'm right here!" Cooper yelled. "I don't know what kind of crap you two are trying to pull, but it's not funny. This ends right now."

Cooper reached for Sage's hand and again it passed right through. He stared at his hands.

Sage shook her head. "He was all I had."

Cooper walked to the window, trying to wrap his brain around the news.

"I'm dead?" he repeated. "How can I be dead?"

Richard stood. "I don't know if this is going to make you feel any better, but that Hart kid is alive, thanks to

Cooper. I guess he had a hole in the foot of his survival suit, and Cooper switched with him at the last minute. Cooper's a hero."

Sage managed a small smile. "He was always my hero."

The electricity blinked a couple of times before calling it quits. Candlelight filled the room.

"You know he's not the only one you had." Richard meet her gaze. "You don't have to be alone tonight." He placed a hand on her arm.

Sage shook her head again and patted Richard's hand. "I'm not alright, Richard, but I'll be okay. Thanks for driving out here and telling me. I know you're a busy man."

"I don't feel right leaving you here alone," protested Richard. "Really, I think I should stay."

"I want to be alone!" blurted Sage. Taking a deep breath, she looked at the deputy. "Please, Richard, I need to digest this in my own way."

"I understand," he said, putting his hat back on. "I'll be back in the morning to check on you. No arguments. Call me if you need anything, and I mean anything."

Sage gave Richard a thankful nod before firmly shutting the door behind him. Cooper watched her pick up Richard's coffee cup, dump it into the sink, and wash it. The candles flickered around her, giving her blonde highlights an amber glow. Setting the cup in the drainer, she made her way to the den and started picking up the scrapbooking material that covered the coffee table. She'd been working on albums for when Cooper came home.

Gathering up the pictures, she came across one of Cooper sitting in a meadow. Wild flowers bloomed all around him as he smiled at her hiding behind the camera.

"I remember that day." Cooper leaned on the mantle. "I didn't want to go, but you said it was a beautiful day, too beautiful to be watching football." A small laugh escaped his mouth. "I will never understand why I made such a fuss about spending the day with you."

Dropping the pictures, she fell to the floor. "Why? Why'd you have to leave me?"

Sage pulled herself onto the couch and curled into a ball. "I told you not to go. I told you it was too dangerous. Why didn't you listen? Why'd you leave me?"

Cooper sprang to the couch, anxious to comfort his love again. "I'm right here, baby. I would never leave you."

He looked around, trying to find a way to show her that he was there. Spotting the candle nearest her, he bent down and concentrated as he blew. The fire went out.

Sage stared at the candle through wet eyes. None of the others had even flickered. Picking up the candle, she examined the wick. It was fine.

Cooper leaned in close, aching to hold her. "I will never leave you again. I promise."

Chapter 1

Cooper watched the box fly out of Sage's hands as she stumbled over an uplifted stone in the walk. He chuckled as she managed to catch herself but could only watch helplessly as all her pillows rolled over the dead winter grass.

"Good thing it was just pillows," Richard said as he set down his own box and started gathering up the pillows.

Sage stood and brushed the grass off her jeans, then sneezed as the dry grass and dust tickled her nose. "As clumsy as I am, I know better than to grab any boxes marked fragile."

Richard hit her with a pillow. "So that's why I'm doing all the heavy lifting? Because you're walking impaired?"

"Hey, you can't blame me for working the system." Sage winked and dodged another swing of the pillow, before bending to help gather pillows. "Thanks again, Richard, for helping me move. Don't think I could've done it alone, and the moving company wanted an arm and a leg."

Richard beat the grass off a pillow. "You know I'm happy to help. Still can't believe you bought this old place." He looked up at the two-story wood cabin nestled on a small hill overlooking Bear Lake before turning his attention to her. "Are you sure you're going to be okay up here by yourself?"

"I'm a big girl. I'll be fine," Sage insisted, pulling her dark blonde hair into a ponytail. "If I can handle the night shift at the hotel, I'm sure I can handle this."

"I'm not talking about the people. I'm sure you could charm the pants off Norman Bates himself." Richard scanned the rest of the property. The place had been abandoned for years and seen better days. "But you really should think about getting a carpenter up here. This place needs work. I can help you with some of it, but most of this stuff needs to be handled by a professional."

"Why, Richard, I do believe you underestimate me and my handyman skills," Sage said in a dramatic southern drawl. Laughing, she continued. "I'm not entirely useless without Coop."

As Sage looked down, Cooper could tell she still had problems saying his name without feeling sad. It made his heart ache for her. He wanted nothing more than to engulf her in a tight embrace. She was just tall enough that her head fit perfectly on his shoulder. Cooper sighed thinking about how he missed having her head rest there. Even as a ghost, it was the only spot where he felt cold.

"It's been a little less than a year, Sage," said Richard. "I can understand you not wanting to live at the house anymore, but maybe you should rent an apartment for a while. At least while you're fixing this place up. My little guest house is still available, cheapest rent in town," Richard fingered a soft cotton pillow before shoving it in the box. "It'll be nice to have a warm roof over your head after working here all day."

Sage shook her head. "I appreciate it, but I'm staying here. Before long, Winter Song will be nice and warm too. Besides, I have every bit of the insurance money and my savings tied up in this place, and yesterday was my last shift at the hotel. I'm ready to rejoin the daylight crowd. Coop and I looked at Winter Song about a dozen times before he left. The inside is outdated, but it's actually in pretty good shape. The electricity works, I've got a solid roof over my head, and I haven't found any rats, which is more than I can say about our last house. He'd be happy I'm following the plan. I don't want to stay any place else."

I'd be happier if I could help you fix the place up, said Cooper. He knew she couldn't hear him, but he still spoke to her often. He hoped there was a part of her that could feel him, or at least sense him being close.

"You know my place is rent free," said Richard. "You don't have to worry about money. I can take care of you."

"As much as I appreciate that, Richard, it's time I took care of myself." She rubbed her arms, the winter breeze causing goose bumps to form. "Besides my place is here. Winter Song is my home now."

"Why'd you name this place Winter Song?" asked Richard. "Wouldn't something like Bear Lake Bed and Breakfast be more appropriate?"

Sage looked at the snowcapped mountains towering over Winter Song, the wind drying the tears from her eyes.

"Coop used to say that when the winter wind barrels through the valley, it sounds like a song. Like the wind is playing winter's song on the mountains," Sage answered.

"We came up with the name a few years ago after one of our visits."

"It's nice. I can see why you went with it. Who knew Cooper was so poetic?"

"Coop wanted everyone to think he was a tough guy," said Sage.

Hey, I am a tough guy!

". . . and I'll be the first to admit he had a temper," she continued, "but he had a good soul. I watched him on a number of occasions help children and animals who couldn't help themselves."

"And I watched him get hauled into jail on a number of occasions too." Richard tried to make it sound like a joke, but Cooper knew better. The deputy had gotten him out of trouble more than a few times.

"Richard, don't." Sage brushed her bangs out of her eyes. "I can never thank you enough for all those times you helped us out, but that's not how I remember Coop. He was a good man."

Thanks, baby, but Richard is right this time. I was a brat with a hot head more times than I'd like to admit. Cooper glanced around the property. *I would give anything to be able to tell you how much I regret those decisions.*

Richard nodded and handed the pillow box to Sage before picking up his own box. "Let's get these inside. You may have pillows, but I think I have a whole library in here."

Sage laughed, causing Cooper to smile.

That's my girl, the bookworm, he said, skimming her hair with his hand.

Sage touched her neck, a small smile forming.

"What are you thinking about?" asked Richard.

Sage shook her head. "Nothing really. Just glad to be finally doing this."

Noah Finnley groaned as he pulled into the driveway and rubbed the back of his neck. Taped on his apartment door was a note, and he knew it wasn't the Avon lady calling. Grabbing his groceries, he headed up the sidewalk, walking slower than needed, hoping the note would morph into something positive. Getting closer, he could just make out the words "Eviction Notice" typed in bold letters across the top of the paper.

"Crap," he muttered under his breath as he read the forty-eight hours' notice. "I really don't need this right now."

The notice wasn't a surprise, since it wasn't the first one to appear on his door. Times had been tough on the young carpenter, since he'd been laid off from the construction company a few months before. People just weren't building, and fewer were renovating. Everyone was pinching pennies, and he was down to his last few.

Noah ripped the notice off the door and went inside. He hated being the kind of person who couldn't pay his bills. It was unnatural to him. He had taken care of his family ever since he was old enough to lift a hammer. He needed a job fast, but first he needed an aspirin for his throbbing head.

Setting the groceries down, he dug in the cabinet over the sink searching for medicine for his headache. Finding the bottle, he gave it a shake and heard nothing. He threw the empty bottle across the room and began to put away his food. He studied his cabinets and groaned. Beans, rice and Romen. His meager grocery budget was definitely putting a damper on his taste buds. He turned to the fridge for better options. Grabbing the milk, he gave it a sniff and grimaced.

"Guess I should've gotten milk at the store," he said to himself as he put the spoiled carton back in the fridge.

Thinking about his options, he shook his head. He was going to have to call his sister. A groan escaped his lips. Asking his sister for help was the last thing he wanted to do. She was taking care of twin girls alone. Although she was making ends meet, he knew she didn't have much to spare. He also knew that she'd give him anything he asked for. Noah shook his head again; there had to be another way.

Grabbing his keys, he headed back out the door. Maybe Buddy at the hardware store would know of someone looking for help. Of course, if that didn't pan out, he could always apply to be a grocery bagger while picking up some milk and aspirin, because neither his money troubles nor his headache were going away without some help.

Chapter 2

Sage waved to Richard as he drove away. Inhaling the strong pine scent of the forest, she released a deep breath. As thankful as she was for Richard's help, she was more thankful to be alone. She'd come to prefer it that way. That was something she'd have to get over whenever guests started to arrive.

"I did it, Coop. I bought this ol' place," Sage whispered as she folded her arms and took in the vast property. Richard was right. It did need a lot of work. "I hope I did the right thing. It won't be easy going it alone."

Well, I can't say I'm not worried, said Cooper, walking up behind her, hands on his hips. *But you'll make it work, baby; you always do. Remember when Richard brought over that woman for dinner, the vegetarian? You'd cooked a pot roast and every vegetable side dish had been soaked in roast juice. She made such a fuss, and Richard suggested we go out, but you wouldn't have it. Before any of us knew what happened, you had eggplant frying in the skillet and a big salad made. If you could make that lady happy, you can make anybody happy.*

Sage leaned on the porch railing and looked over her shoulder at the pine porch swing. She walked to the chair and examined the rough old ropes that attached the seat to the porch ceiling, giving each one a sturdy tug.

"I wonder if it'll hold?" she asked the air.

There's only one way to find out. Cooper grinned. *Of course if it doesn't, you're the one who's gonna fall on your butt.*

Sage turned and slowly lowered herself onto the swing. It creaked a little, but held steady. The cushions were well worn and Sage could feel the wood under the fabric as she relaxed.

Cooper settled in beside her. *I've always loved this place, and I love you. I'm so happy you're doing this.* He reached for her hand and sighed as his passed through hers. *One day I'll be able to hold this hand again . . . one day.*

Smiling, Sage started swinging back and forth. "I think it's gonna hold."

The porch swing creaked one last protest before she felt the seat drop from beneath her, causing her rear to hit the ground.

"Or not." Sage rolled her eyes as she looked at the porch ceiling. "Guess it's time to start that to-do list."

Standing up, she dusted herself off, studied the broken rope, and looked towards the barn. "I bet there's more rope in there, maybe even some chain." Sage shook her head. "Girl, you've got to stop talking to yourself like this. Do that in front of Richard or some customer, and they're gonna think you're off your rocker."

Hopping down the porch stairs, Sage made her way to the barn. She had only been in the barn one other time. It was the first time she and Cooper had looked at the place. They'd been high school sweethearts fresh from graduation. She planned on going to school and getting her degree in travel and hospitality, while Cooper did all the hands-on repairs. They were both full of optimism and hope with a lifetime ahead of them.

The house itself wasn't worth much anymore. Built in the late 70's, it needed a major renovation to bring it up to style. It was the land by the lake where Winter Song sat that kept the price out of reach of the two lovebirds. Instead of going to college, Sage started working as a maid at the hotel, learning about the hospitality industry from the ground up. Cooper took any job he could find in construction, learning a trade that would one day make their dreams of Winter Song a reality.

While Sage made her way up the hospitality industry ladder, from maid to desk clerk, then to night manager. Cooper bounced from seasonal job to seasonal job. She remembered the day he came in saying he'd been hired onto the *Fancy Nancy*, a cod boat out of Seattle, Washington. In fact she remembered it as if it were yesterday.

"Are you nuts?" she had screamed. "We both watched that documentary on TV. It's dangerous. It's cold. It's dangerous. Its hours upon hours of no sleep. Oh, and did I mention it's one of the most dangerous job on the face of the planet?"

"Baby, come on. One season on the boat, and we'll have our down payment for Winter Song. Once we get the B&B up and running, we can work our own hours. Decide our own fate. Finally get married." He hugged her tight and nuzzled her hair. "I need to make an honest woman out of you."

"You want an honest woman?" she asked, knocking his arms off and pacing across the room. "Well, let me be honest. I don't want you to go. I think it's a dangerous and stupid decision. We'll get the money some other way." She threw up her arms. "You don't even like to fish."

Cooper rolled his eyes. "Babe, you're overreacting. Nothing's gonna happen to me."

"You do realize you won't be able to quit once you're out there?" Sage asked. "If you get mad at your boss or coworkers, you can't just walk off the site. You'll be stuck."

"I'm not looking to quit. I can finally see the finish line, and if the finish line requires me to spend time on a boat with five or six smelly men, then so be it. You're acting like I'm being selfish."

"You are!" Sage yelled. "You haven't given one thought about how I feel about this. How this affects us."

"Is that so?" Cooper yelled back. "I'm doing this for us. For you and me. How is that selfish? How is that not thinking about us?"

"Because you're putting your life in danger for something we can accomplish without a season on a cod boat." She wrapped her arms around him. "I'll work two jobs if it means keeping you safe. Please don't go. It isn't worth the risk. We'll do it another way."

"It's too late, Sage." Cooper shook his head. "I've signed the contract and faxed it back. I leave in a couple of days."

"Without talking to me first?" She bit her lip as tears filled her eyes. "Coop, if anything happens to you . . . I just don't know what I'd do." She buried her head in his shoulder. "You know, I'll never let you live it down."

He lifted her chin so her eyes met his. "Nothing is going to happen to me, and if it does, I will gladly listen to a lifetime of *I told you so*." He kissed her gently.

Sage shook the memory away before it could go any further. Wrapping her arms around her shoulders she whispered, "I told you so."

Cooper shook his head. The stubborn girl had said it a million times since that snowy night at the house. He was sure she'd say it a million times more. Shaking his head, he thought he saw something peek its head out of the open barn door.

Hold on, Sage, he said holding his arm out. She walked through it. Cursing, he ran ahead of her to the barn. He'd learned how to blow out candles and move a few small objects, but he still couldn't physically touch a person. Closing his eyes, he walked through the door. He flinched every time he walked through a wall, still not used to the awkward sensation.

There in the dark he heard a low, guttural sound. It didn't take long for his eyes to find the source. A brown and white dog with tall ears stood in the corner, staring directly at Cooper.

Okay, puppy, be cool, said Cooper, walking towards the dog. *I'm not gonna hurt you. I just need to talk to you for a second.*

The dog growled a little louder and bared its front teeth.

It's okay. I'm glad you can see me. Maybe you could do me a favor? Cooper whispered to the dog. *You bark really loudly so that nice lady can hear you and run away. She doesn't bother you, and you don't bite her. Doesn't that sound like a good deal? What do you say? Wanna be friends? Come on, be a good puppy. Speak!*

The dog turned its attention to the door.

Crap. Cooper ran toward the dog shouting, *over here you mangy mutt. Stay away from her!*

Chapter 3

The animal ignored Cooper and shot towards the door as Sage pulled it open. She screamed as the beast charged, but she didn't run. The dog stopped ten feet from her, barking and snarling. Sage took a couple of steps back as the dog stepped forward.

"Easy there," Sage said in a calm voice, placing her hands in front of her. "I'm not gonna hurt you. I get it. You were here first. This is your home. I'll back off."

She continued to back away from the dog, studying its characteristics. The dog was definitely a female and had large ears that stood upright and alert, just like a jackrabbit. Its brown and white spots told her the dog was probably a blue heeler mix. The farther Sage backed, the less the dog barked.

Cooper let out a sigh of relief as Sage retreated all the way to the house, and the dog didn't follow. He was sure she'd call Richard to come take care of it.

Cooper cringed at the thought. Of course Richard would have to take care of it, because he was no longer able too. A helpless feeling sank into his gut. Nothing felt worse than not being able to help Sage when she really needed it.

Finding herself safe on the porch, Sage debated her next step. The dog now walked around the barn, making sure there were no other intruders. Was it really fair to have the dog hauled off, or worse, just because she had decided to buy the place?

What are you doing? asked Cooper. *Go inside and call Richard. That dog could be rabid. And even if it's not, it's not safe. That devil dog is gonna bite someone.*

Sage brushed her hands off and walked inside.

Finally! said Cooper. *Why does it always take you so long to realize I'm right?*

Walking to the phone in the kitchen, she picked up the receiver. No dial tone. Mentally slapping herself on the forehead, she put the receiver back in its cradle. It wouldn't be installed until the next day.

Grabbing her cell phone, she searched for a signal. No bars. She knew that would be an issue when she bought the place, but she didn't like cell phones anyway, and her customers would be here to "get away from it all," so it was a nonissue as long as the land line worked.

Just get in the jeep and go get Richard, said Cooper. *You should've waited until the phone line was put in place before moving out here.*

Sage sighed. The dog would get to keep the barn for now. She opened a box and took out a tall plastic glass. A cool drink of mountain water was just what she needed.

The pipes groaned as she turned the cold water knob. Nothing came out. Setting her cup down, she turned the hot water knob. The pipes groaned again, but still no water. Sage clicked her fingernails on the countertop and stared at the faucet. The realtor had told her the pipes were fine in the dusty old place. The plumbing and electrical wiring were both up to code. Winter Song had been inspected before she bought it.

The pipes let out one final groan before spewing water into the sink. Sage reached out and turned off the hot, then tried to do the same with the cold water only to have the knob come off in her hand.

"You've got to be kidding me," she said, looking from the knob to the water rushing from the faucet. "Well, at least it's all going down the sink."

You better turn off the main valve, Cooper leaned against the counter. *Might have some pressure built up, and I don't think that faucet was attached properly.*

The pipes groaned again as the main spigot shot off, causing a geyser of water. Sage screamed as the frigid spring water hit her face.

Told ya. Cooper snickered.

Wiping her wet hair out of her eyes, she reached under the sink and turned off the water line. The geyser slowed to a gurgle and then stopped.

Scanning the kitchen, she spotted a box of towels at the other end of the large room. As she turned toward the box, she slipped in a puddle, her feet sliding out from under her as her rear hit the ground for a second time that day.

"You've got to be freakin' kidding me," Sage said, again rubbing her backside.

Cooper's laugh filled the kitchen. *You are by far the clumsiest person I've ever met. I'd help you up if I could.*

Sage groaned as she lifted herself out of the cold water. "Guess I'll just add mopping to the list of things to do, 'cause that list obviously isn't long enough."

Slowly making her way across the room, she finally grabbed a towel and dried her face. "First the porch swing falls, then there's a rabid dog in the barn and now a flood in the kitchen. What else could possibly go wrong?"

Oh, you don't want to say that. Cooper shook his head still laughing.

Sage moved the towel to her hair as a bolt of lightning flashed through the sky followed by a loud clap of thunder causing her to jump.

"Pull yourself together, Sage. It's just a thunderstorm," she chastised herself as the rain began to fall. "You've got a warm, mostly dry home over your head. You'll be fine, lots of unpacking to do."

No sooner had she said the words than she felt something drip on her head. She glanced up in time to catch a drop of water in her eye.

"Seriously?" she said to the ceiling. "Are you freakin' kidding me?"

Sage hustled around the kitchen gathering pots and pans to catch the water dripping from the ceiling. When she finally finished, she sat in the middle of the floor and pulled the towel tightly around her shoulders.

"No one said it would be easy," she muttered to herself.

Closing her eyes, she listened to the rain as Cooper snuggled up behind her. She tried to clear her mind, to just enjoy the soft percussion of nature, but her memory had other ideas. Before she could stop herself, she could see Cooper.

He was running in front of her, gently pulling her along as they ran through the rain. Sage smiled at the memory. They were barely twenty, and the world was theirs to conquer. As they reached the porch of the one-bedroom cabin that was their first home together, Sage pulled Cooper toward her and kissed him in the rain.

"I've always dreamed about doing that," she said, smiling.

"Baby, I'll make all your dreams come true." Cooper smiled back, before kissing her again. "Now come on, it's cold."

He pulled her inside where they shed their raincoats and boots. Sage hurried to the kitchen. "I'll make us some omelets and hot cocoa. That'll warm us up."

As she gathered the necessary ingredients for their brunch from the fridge, Cooper switched on the stereo. The soft melody of their song caressed the air, and Sage began to sway to the music. Soon she felt Cooper's strong arms wrap around her as he hugged her from behind. She leaned into him as he kissed her neck, then giggled as he nibbled on her ear.

She set the eggs back in the fridge and turned around to face her lover. She kissed him, giving his bottom lip a quick bite, causing Cooper to give her a wicked smile. Pushing her against the fridge, they locked hands as he kissed her hard on the lips before moving back to her neck.

"Stop it, Sage!" she yelled, bringing herself out of her daydream. "Those kinds of memories are not helpful right now. He's never coming back. It's time to move forward." She brushed a tear off her cheek.

Baby, said Cooper, *it'll be okay. I wish we had more than memories. But we still have a lifetime. I'm here, I'll always be here.*

Sage got up and started unpacking more kitchen boxes.

Dammit, said Cooper, *I'd give anything to let you know I'm still here.*

He looked around the room before focusing on a small pan catching one of the many leaks. Bending over it, he concentrated. The pan shook a little before flipping over.

Sage screamed, looking around the room. Seeing nothing, she walked to the pan and examined it. "Cooper, was that you?"

She laughed at herself before frowning. "Of course, it wasn't. In fact it couldn't have been you . . . You're dead."

Chapter 4

Burying his head under the pillow, Noah tried to stifle the noise of someone banging on his door, but it wouldn't stop. Glancing at the clock, he groaned at the 7:30 a.m. wake up call. The knocking increased.

Rolling over onto his back, he weighed his options. More than likely, it was his landlady kicking him out. He could face it now and open the door like a civilized person, or he could wait for Mrs. Murphy to unlock the door and come barging into his bedroom. Either way his dream of sleeping in wasn't going to happen.

Sighing, Noah sat up and reached for his pants. No way was he going to let Mrs. Murphy see him in his boxers. She was the kind to think of an alternative payment for his past due rent. He shuddered at the thought. Maybe though, just maybe, he'd be able to talk her into some extended time.

Shuffling to the door, he took a deep breath and plastered fake smile on his face before turning the doorknob. "Mrs. Murphy, how delightful to see you this fine morning."

His mouth dropped open as a stunning blonde, highlights glinting in the sun, stared at him. Looking down at a small purple Post-it note, she raised an eyebrow before speaking. "Are you Noah Finnley?"

Come on, Sage, you aren't really thinking of hiring this guy? Cooper said from behind her. *I mean, look at him. What kind of carpenter isn't awake at 7:30 a.m.?*

Noah rubbed his jaw and neck. He could see the woman sizing him up. His strong jaw line gave way to a slender neck, sitting on tan broad shoulders. His bronze pecs gave witness to hours spent outside without his shirt on. Remembering his manners, he grabbed a wadded up t-shirt.

"Sorry, 'bout that," said Noah, trying to smooth out the wrinkles. "Yes, I'm Noah Finnley. What can I do for you, umm . . . sorry, I didn't catch your name."

That's because she didn't say it, pal, grumbled Cooper.

Sage extended her hand. "Sage McKennan."

Noah accepted the hand. "What can I do for you, Mrs. McKennan?"

Sage flinched. "It's Mi--please just call me Sage. I'm looking for a jack-of-all-trades and was given your number and address at the hardware store. They said you've been looking for work, and that you know what you're doing. I tried to call the number, but all I got was a message saying it had been disconnected. Sorry to come by so early, but the forecast calls for more storms tonight, and I have a roof in desperate need of repair . . . among other things."

Noah studied Sage. The way her lush pink lips formed a small pout as she waited for his decision made him lick his own parched lips.

Sage, this guy's only thinking about one thing, and it ain't your roof, said Cooper.

"Look," said Sage, "there's a lot of work to be done at Winter Song …"

"Winter Song?" Noah interrupted.

"Yeah, it's the ol' Ritter place down by the lake. I'm converting it into a bed and breakfast and calling it Winter Song. Didn't think 'The Ol' Ritter Place' would attract many tourists." She smiled at her own joke.

Perked up at the word "bed," didn't ya, fella? Cooper sneered. *Don't even think about it, pal. This girl's not on the market.*

"I don't think I'm your man." Noah tried to shut the door on her, silently cursing having to turn down the job. But he could tell this job came with strings. He had seen this type of thing before and didn't want anything to do with working for a woman with the type of strings Sage was tangled up in. It would get messy and knotted, and he'd have to leave the job anyway, more than likely without pay.

Sage placed a hand on the door and held it open. "Okay, so I'm not funny, but you haven't even heard my proposition."

You heard the man, Sage, urged Cooper. *He doesn't want the job. Let's go.*

"Proposition?" Noah let go of the door. "I thought it would be an 'I do the work, you pay me' kind of situation." Noah furrowed his brow.

"More of a partnership really. You see most of my money is tied up in fixing Winter Song. I have enough to live on and for the supplies needed to fix the place, but not actually enough to pay someone what they're worth to do those necessary repairs. The man at the hardware store said you might need some place to stay. I have a barn you can fix up and live in rent free. Of course, we'll have to get the dog out of it first."

"Dog?" said Noah, raising an eyebrow.

Cooper leaned into Noah. *I'm pretty sure you've been called a dog before, so you're familiar with the phrase.*

"Yeah, she's a stray and a bit, let's see, how do I put this?" Sage tapped her finger on her chin. ". . . protective of the barn, and I'm afraid if I called anyone, they'd just go out and shoot her. I can't have them shooting a dog because of me, so I'll have to befriend her. But you can stay in the main house until I get the barn dog-free and while you're fixing it up."

Cooper threw his hands up in the air. *Great, Sage, I can already see what he's thinking. Listen, pal, if you think you're gonna sneak down the hall and be with my girl, think again.* Cooper poked his finger at Noah's chest.

Noah narrowed his eyebrows and looked directly at Cooper. "Watch it."

Cooper jerked his finger back. *You can see me?*

Sage raised an eyebrow at Noah.

"I thought I saw a bee," said Noah, turning his attention back to Sage. "And what do I do about food and my other expenses?"

Cooper waved his hands in front of Noah's face. *I swear you looked right at me.*

Noah didn't blink. Cooper ran his hands through his hair. *I could've sworn he was talking to me.*

"Food, I'll provide as part of the payment for fixing up the place." Sage answered Noah. "Of course, any supplies you need for Winter Song will come out of the business account. If you have a paying job come up, we'll work out a time schedule so you can do both. I'm pretty flexible."

Noah shook his head. "I don't know."

"Once Winter Song is up and running, I'll give you a salary plus let you continue to live in the barn if you stay on as my handyman." Sage looked at Noah, her dark blue eyes begging for an answer.

Oh, crap, you're toast, said Cooper. *No one can resist that look.*

Noah shook his head again. "This is a bad idea."

"Why?" asked Sage. "The guy at the hardware store was pretty blunt about your situation. As I understand it, if you don't leave this house today, Mrs. Murphy's going to throw you out and confiscate your stuff."

See, that's what happens to deadbeats, said Cooper.

"I know the guy shouldn't have told me about your situation," continued Sage, "but he said you're a good guy and that we could help each other. Looks to me like a win-win situation. Just give me one good reason why not, and I'll leave you alone."

Noah rubbed his jaw as he saw Mrs. Murphy pull up in her blue station wagon, papers in hand. It didn't take a rocket scientist to know it was an order to vacate the premises. Running his hands through his tawny hair, he nodded his head.

"I guess you've got yourself a handyman," said Noah, extending his hand.

Sage shook it before starting toward her Jeep. "You won't regret this, Mr. Finnley."

"I doubt that," Noah mumbled under his breath.

"What?" asked Sage, turning around.

"Call me Noah," he replied. "Just give me a couple of hours to gather my stuff, and I'll be out there to take a look at what we'll need to get us through the night." Noah waved to Mrs. Murphy, who stood nearby.

Oh, look, he's already talking about getting you through the night. What did I tell you, Sage? said Cooper. *Guys like that only think of one thing.*

"Great!" Sage smiled. "I'll leave you to take care of your business with Mrs. Murphy." She turned back towards her Jeep. "Thanks again, Noah."

Noah watched Sage drive away and shook his head. "This is a mistake," he mumbled before turning his attention to Mrs. Murphy.

Chapter 5

Sage turned the flank steaks on the grill and closed the lid. They were almost ready. Her mouth watered as the smell drifted to her nose causing her stomach to growl. Skipping breakfast was a bad idea, but she had been anxious to get to Noah before he left town.

I can't believe you're fixing that man a steak, sneered Cooper. *It's sending the wrong message.*

Returning to the grill, Sage forked one of the steaks onto a plate.

On the other hand, maybe he won't get the wrong idea if you give him a steak that's mooing, Cooper continued.

Sage hopped down the steps and headed to the barn.

Crap. Sage, you are not going to feed that dog. Cooper followed. *This is a bad idea. That dog will kill you, eat the steak, and then eat you.*

Slowing as she approached the barn, Sage whistled lowly. "Here puppy, puppy."

Puppy? Cooper grunted. *Yeah, if that dog is a puppy then Cujo was a bunny rabbit. Sage, let's be smart about this. Turn around and go back to the house.*

Sage heard a low growl from the doorway. "It's okay, puppy," she cooed. "I brought you a nice warm steak. I didn't know how you liked it, so I cooked it rare. I promise I didn't poison it. I want to be your friend."

Cooper tilted his head. *Actually, that's not a bad idea for the dog or the slob you hired. Just give them both a little laxative in their meals, and before long both will be on their merry little ways. No harm, no foul, except for the smell.*

She bent down and placed the plate on the ground. "I'll just leave this here, and you can eat it whenever you like. I'm gonna go back up to the house and eat mine. You can have my scraps when I'm finished."

Standing up, she backed away from the barn. With each step back, the dog took a step forward, its nose high in the air sniffing the savory aroma. As soon as Sage was safe on the porch, the dog grabbed the steak and ran back into the barn.

Sage brushed her hands off and forked her steak off the grill. Sitting on the step, plate in her lap, she began to devour her brunch.

Cooper licked his lips. *I'm not even hungry, but I'd kill for a bite of that right now.*

He sat by his love and studied her face. *You must be worried about that Noah guy,* he mumbled, then looked up at the porch ceiling. *Your eyes always go a shade darker when you're worried, almost black when you're mad. I should know, I made you mad and worried you enough times.* He looked back at Sage and watched her blot her lips with a napkin. *That steak isn't the only thing I'd kill for. I miss kissing you more than I miss eating. Your touch is the only thing I still hunger for.*

Sage sighed as she got up and walked back toward the barn. As she reached the door, she prepared herself for a growl. There was none. "I hope the lack of growling means your mouth is too full to bite me," Sage joked. "Here's my leftovers as promised. Bon appétit."

She threw the scraps on the ground and turned. Hearing a rustling she spun around. The dog stood in the doorway, a chunk of meat in her mouth.

"Hey, puppy," said Sage in a light tone.

Be careful, Sage. Cooper reached out, just in case he needed to pull Sage back. Realizing he couldn't pull her back no matter the danger, he sighed and dropped his arms.

Bending down, she reached out her hand. "Want to be friends? I need a good guard dog, and by the looks of it, you need some good meals. It won't be steak all the time, but I promise not to buy the cheap dog food."

The dog growled and retreated into the barn. Sage stood and rubbed her hands on her jeans. "I'll win you over, puppy. Just wait; you'll see."

Sage turned her attention to the road as a police truck inched its way toward Winter Song. She waved at Richard as he pulled up beside her.

"Just wanted to see how you're settling in," he said, his wrist resting on the steering wheel. "Any problems yesterday?"

Sage and Cooper laughed. *Deputy Park, you don't even want to know,* said Cooper.

"Where do I begin?" sighed Sage.

"What's wrong?" Richard turned off the truck and got out.

"Well," Sage said with a big sigh, "the bad news is there was a geyser in the kitchen, the roof leaks, and the porch swing fell while I was sitting on it."

"Ouch," said Richard.

Tell him about the dog, Cooper encouraged. *Maybe he can talk some sense into you and get rid of the mutt.*

"Sadly enough, it wasn't the only time my butt hit the ground yesterday."

Richard turned to Sage. "I don't like this. You aren't safe out here alone."

Sage laughed. "The only person I have to worry about is myself. Besides I'm not going to be out here alone any more. I took your advice and hired a handyman this morning."

"That was fast. Who?" asked Richard, lifting up his cowboy hat to scratch his head.

A real chump if you ask me, Richard. The guy was getting kicked out of his apartment this morning, and now Sage wants to hire him? Come on, you've got to talk her out of it, explained Cooper. *I've tried, not that she can hear me, but you've got to make her be sensible.*

"His name is Noah Finnley. Heard of him?" Sage leaned against the truck.

"Was he staying in Mrs. Murphy's rental?" asked Richard.

Oh great, it's worse than we thought. He's got a rap sheet. I just knew it. Cooper kicked at the dirt, causing a few pebbles to move.

"Yes," answered Sage. "Is he a problem?"

"I'm not sure," said Richard. "Mrs. Murphy just came in this morning stating she was evicting him today. She didn't think he'd be a problem, but she always lets me know before she kicks someone out, just in case. Are you sure you want to hire someone who can't pay his rent? He's got no place to live."

"He does now," said Sage.

"And what does that mean?" Richard folded his arms.

"He's gonna stay here," answered Sage, avoiding Richard's glare. "I've got more than enough room, and I can't afford to pay any handyman what they're worth, so room and board are part of the deal."

Richard's mouth dropped. "When I told you to find someone, this was not what I had in mind. You've got no idea who this guy is. For all you know, he could rob you blind. This isn't a smart idea, Sage."

Finally, a voice of reason she can actually hear. Cooper threw his hands up and looked at the sky. *Please talk some sense into this crazy girl.*

"Settle down, Richard." Sage folded her arms. "Look, he was desperate for a job and place to stay. I'm desperate for a handyman, but I don't have the money to pay for the labor. The guy at the hardware store highly recommended him, so I don't think he's gonna 'rob me blind'. As soon as we get the feral dog out of the barn, he'll fix that up and live there. Until then, he can stay in one of the guest rooms. We can't open until spring anyway. I'd say, given the circumstances, this is a pretty smart idea. I have someone to help me fix things up, and I'm not out here all alone."

"I don't know." Richard shook his head. "Wait, did you say feral dog?"

Thank God, I know Richard won't let that dog stay here. Tell him about the devil dog. Cooper crossed his arms and leaned on the police truck. *I'm so glad you're here. Someone needs to tell her she's making a huge mistake not getting rid of the mutt.*

Sage twirled a lock of hair around her finger, then jerked her hand away, silently cursing the childhood habit that made her look like a school girl. "Yes, after the porch swing broke, I went to the barn to look for some more rope or chain. That's when I met the dog."

"Get to the feral part, Sage," said Richard, eyeing the barn.

"It's just that I don't think she's been around many people while living out here. I think I might have scared her."

"Did she bite you?" Richard placed a hand on his gun.

"No," said Sage, grabbing his hand. "She just growled at me, and I took that as a hint she didn't want me there, so I left the barn. I just fed her a steak. She'll warm up to me in no time. She's a harmless stray, Richard, so honestly there's no reason to fuss."

Says the girl who was going to call Animal Control yesterday, Cooper snarled.

"Why don't you let me check the situation out and see for myself," said Richard, taking a step toward the barn.

Sage pulled him back. "I have a better idea. Instead of bothering the dog, whom I'm trying to befriend, why don't you let me show you the house instead?"

Richard raised an eyebrow. "I don't like this, Sage. There could be a number of things wrong with that dog."

"And I appreciate your concern, Richard. I promise if I have any problems with the dog or the handyman, I'll call you straight away."

Richard nodded. "You promise?"

Sage held up three fingers in a Girl Scout promise pledge. "I promise. Now come on, you're never gonna believe the hardwood floors in here. They're almost perfect."

Chapter 6

She smiled and released a deep breath as Richard's truck disappeared down the hill just as Noah's black truck appeared over it. Even though he had agreed to help, she was still afraid Noah wouldn't show up.

Having someone to help fix up the place was one thing, not being alone was another. Without fail, every moment alone was time spent thinking about Cooper. It hadn't helped that Winter Song had been just as much his dream as it was hers.

She had considered, on a number of occasions, buying a different bed and breakfast. Wyoming had no shortage of beautiful cabins for sale, just waiting for an owner. But she couldn't let go of Winter Song, even if it brought back memories. She had to take a chance on the dream they'd shared. If Cooper's death had taught her anything, it was that life was short. The last thing she wanted was to regret not buying the place they fell in love with together.

She'd spent the last half hour convincing Richard she was safe with Noah around. Truth was, she knew nothing about Noah other than what the hardware clerk had told her, but she'd have to trust him to get the work done. At this moment, she had no other choice.

Noah brought his truck to a stop and stepped out. He had cleaned up from that morning, His shirt, no longer wrinkled, barely contained the arm muscles of a man who had worked hard all of his life. His sandy hair was still tousled, but Sage got the feeling that was just his look.

She approached him. "I'm so glad you came."

I'm not. Cooper studied Noah, who earlier at the apartment had seemed to look right at him. Cooper shrugged it off as a coincidence, but the moment still played in his head.

"I said I'd come," said Noah. "I'm a man of my word."

"That's what Buddy at the hardware store said, but if you get a look at this place and change your mind, I'll understand." Sage bit her lip. "There's a lot of work to be done."

Cooper smiled. *That's right, baby, give him a way out.*

"Are you having second thoughts about me being able to do the work?" asked Noah.

"Not at all," answered Sage. "It's just some might question the nature of our arrangement given your circumstances this morning. I really don't know that much about you."

Cooper stepped in front of Sage. *Except that you're a deadbeat who skips out on past rent, leaving people high and dry.*

"I'm a carpenter by trade, but I know my way around most electric and plumbing systems. I grew up in Montana building traditional houses and log cabins with my uncle. I had a steady job with the same company for a long time, but people aren't building like they used to. The company went under, and I found myself unemployed. I will pay Mrs. Murphy her back rent when I can. I don't leave debts unpaid." His eyes got hard as he looked toward her, but Sage got the impression he wasn't really looking at her at all.

"Now, if you're satisfied," he continued, "I'd like to get started." Noah eyed the barn. Although worn by the weather and years gone by, it appeared to be quite sturdy. "You said there is a stray dog in there?"

Sage nodded. "Yeah, but I'm working on her. We should probably start with the house." She picked up the dog's discarded plate. "Let's go in through the back door. The porch needs some work. I'm afraid if anyone leans on the railing, it'll fall." She pointed to the swing. "Let me tell you, it's not fun."

Noah chuckled. "I take it you took the swing for a test run?"

"Yeah, good times," said Sage, stepping onto the porch.

Noah followed, turned, and whistled. "Quite a view you have here. I'm surprised this old place wasn't bought years ago."

Cooper smirked. *I know what view you're whistling at, pal.*

"Paul Ritter's son wouldn't sell it to anyone who wasn't local. Said his dad would roll over in his grave if they put a big resort or something like that up here," Sage answered.

He's probably rolling over in his grave right now knowing you're the one fixing up his place. Cooper jammed his hands in his pockets. *A drifter slash carpenter mooching off a poor single woman.*

"But he's okay with you making it into a B&B?" asked Noah.

"Yeah, he said his father was happiest when his house was full." Sage looked out over the crystal blue water of Bear Lake. "Once the house and barn are done, I'd like to build a small dock out there for canoes."

Cooper inched close to Noah's ear. *I bet a two-bit hack like you can't even fix a door knob much less build a dock. I bet you're nothing but a lazy, good for nothing, son of a...*

"Enough." Noah jerked his head and met Cooper eye to eye.

Cooper knew this time it was no coincidence. The handyman knew he was there, but he still wasn't sure how much Noah could see or hear. *Are you talking to me?*

"I'm sorry," said Sage, looking confused. "Enough what?"

"I appreciate the offer of a tour," he said, still staring a Cooper. "But if you don't mind I'd like to take a look at the roof first, so I can get it done before the storm tonight. Once it hits, we'll have time to go over the rest of your list."

Cooper's mouth stood open as Noah looked at Sage, breaking the staring contest.

"Don't you want to see where you're staying?" asked Sage.

Noah shook his head. "I'll be sleeping in the barn."

"Oh, you can't!" Sage laid her hand on Noah's arm causing Cooper to flinch. "What if that dog bites you? I'll never forgive myself. There's plenty of room inside. I insist."

Cooper tried to make eye contact with Noah again. *You can see me?*

Noah turned his attention back to Cooper. "We'll talk about it later."

Are you talking to her or me? Cooper asked. *What's going on here?*

"Well, okay," said Sage, nodding. "I'll leave you to your work, but we're not finished with this discussion."

Noah watched Sage go through the kitchen door before turning to Cooper.

"I'm talking to you," Noah said under his breath as he headed for his truck. "Meet me on the roof."

Noah grumbled as he unlatched his tailgate and reached for the ladder. "I should drive away right now. I finally find work, and it comes with a ghost. Why can't they just go into the stupid light?" he mumbled. "I knew better than to come out here. The minute she arrived at my doorstep with him in tow, I should've run the other direction."

Leaning the ladder against the house, Noah took a quick detour up the porch and peeked his head into the kitchen. Sage looked up and smiled. "Change your mind about the tour?"

"Um." Noah scratched his head. "No, this is going to sound weird, but I'm going on the roof now, and you might hear me talking to myself."

Sage giggled. "Not weird at all. There will be times you'll hear me talking to myself too. You know, working out where to put stuff."

Noah slapped the door frame. "Okay then, I'll make a list of what we need to get the roof in shape, then head to town."

Leaving Sage in the kitchen, Noah walked to the ladder. Taking a deep breath, he made his way up onto the roof where he found Cooper pacing.

"Can you touch people?" Noah asked.

Cooper threw his hands up in the air. *Are you serious? I finally find someone who can see me, and you want to know if I can touch people?*

"Well, can you?"

Cooper sighed. *No, but I'm working on it. Why?*

"Just want to make sure you're not going to push me off this roof," said Noah, walking the roof and checking the shingles. "Who are you?"

My name is Cooper Davis, and why would I push you off this roof when you're the only one in this podunk town that can see or hear me? Cooper started to pace.

"And how are you related to Sage?" asked Noah, bending to study another shingle.

Well, technically we aren't related, but she's been my girl since middle school.

Noah stood. "And how long have you been haunting her?"

Haunting her? I'm not haunting her. I don't go around wearing sheets and clanking chains. I love her, and I promised I would never leave her again. I've kept that promise for almost a year.

"You're the guy who died in the Bering Sea when that cod boat sank, aren't you?" asked Noah. "You saved that boy."

I guess so, but that doesn't really matter now. Cooper continued to pace. *This is great. I don't even know where to start.* He ran his fingers through his hair and rubbed his hands together. *Of course, we'll start with you telling Sage how much I mi . . . .*

Noah held up his hand. "Don't."

Don't what? asked Cooper.

"Don't ask me to go down there and relay a message to Sage or anybody else. I ain't the ghost whisperer you've seen on TV or read about in books. Messages like that just cause grief and heartache to be stirred up. I understand you're a hero and that you and Sage have a long past, but it's time for you to go into the light."

Noah pointed to the chimney. A bright white light started as a sliver and grew until it was a large glowing doorway the size of the chimney. "It's right there. You'll find peace there, and I'm sure you have some family waiting to meet you."

Sage is my family, and I'm hers! yelled Cooper. *She's the only family I've had for a long time, and she begged me not to leave her before I got on that God-forsaken boat. I made her a promise that I'd never leave her alone again, and I intend to keep that promise. I can't imagine not being able to see the only girl I've ever loved. I watch her sitting alone on the porch of our dream home, her hair twinkling in the sunlight, and I just want to run my fingers through it. But I can't! And now you're telling me you won't even tell her I'm here. That I've been by her side ever since I died?*

Noah ignored Cooper. "You'll find peace in the light, and Sage will find her peace here."

Cooper closed the distance between them. *Is that what you intend to do? Help Sage find 'peace'? That's why you want me to go into the light, so you can have her all to yourself.*

"I'm just here to do a job, nothing more." Noah clenched his teeth. "You can't have her. Don't you get that? You're dead. You can't do anything for her. You staying here is just causing her pain."

Look, I'm not going into that light, so you can turn it off. I know she wants me here. You're the one who wants me gone. And that ain't gonna happen, pal.

The light disappeared.

Cooper turned to Noah. *Does this mean you'll talk to Sage for me?*

Noah shook his head. "I have no control over the light. It appears when I'm talking to a ghost. It'll keep showing up no matter how stubborn you are. And no, I will not be relaying any messages to Sage. She's doing good, getting on with her life, and you're just going to screw it all up."

Cooper jabbed his finger in Noah's face. *Listen closely, pal. You will talk to Sage for me, or I'll make your life a living hell.*

"It already is."

Chapter 7

Sage glanced at the ceiling. She couldn't believe it, Noah really was having a conversation with himself. Could the roof really be that bad? She found only six leaks the night before and all in the dining room. Praying she wouldn't need to replace the entire roof, Sage set a small bouquet of peonies on the kitchen bar.

She picked off a couple of ants on the thick, pink, blooms and looked around the room. The large kitchen overlooked the open living and dining spaces with their tall slanted ceilings. She pictured her guests sitting around the bar talking about how they pulled in a big trout while fly fishing or came across a moose while hiking as she cooked up a hearty breakfast or fun snack.

Three cozy tables would sit in the corner by one of the big picture windows overlooking the lake, giving her guests dining privacy, while comfy chairs and a sofa would face the glorious pine trees and mountains on the other side of the room. No matter which window her guests looked through, Winter Song had an awe-inspiring view. Even the three bedrooms on the second floor just above her office, the master bedroom, and small den had views that would make Van Gogh cry.

Her heart fluttered at the thought of a house filled with people. It was both exciting and scary. Actually living with the guests would be nothing like working the front desk at the hotel. She'd be cooking breakfast and dinner, along with picnic lunches that could be purchased every day. There would be piles of sheets, towels, and other linens to be washed daily, not to mention that cleaning this giant place would be a huge chore in itself. She shook her head.

Cooper appeared by her side.

Can you believe that guy? He motioned to the roof. *I finally find someone who can talk to you. Someone who can really let you know I'm here--that I haven't left, and he won't do it. I just want to punch him right in the face.*

"I don't think I can do this alone, Coop," Sage said, looking up to the sky. "It was always our dream. This is not a job for one person. Who am I kidding?" She slumped down in an oversized chair. "I might as well go to the bank and tell them it was all a big mistake. If I go right now, I bet I can even get my job back at the hotel and rent Richard's guest house. That really is the smart thing to do. I'm in way over my head here."

Oh, honey, no. Cooper walked behind Sage and gently grazed her hair. *You'd always get this way before every new adventure.* He laughed. *Come to think about it, you'd get this way before every dinner party, even though they were always a smashing success. You succeed in everything you put your mind to, and you'll be great at this too.*

Cooper looked up at the roof and groaned. *If only that pig-headed jerk up there would talk to you for me!*

Sage sat up and squared her shoulders. "No, I can do this. I am not alone. I have Noah to help out. I'll be fine."

Cooper groaned again. *That loser won't lift a finger to help. He's already proven that.*

Slapping her knees, Sage stood up. "I can do this," she said again.

"Do what?"

Sage let out a squeak as Noah let himself in the back door. "Noah, you scared me. I'm so used to being alone. I just about forgot you were here."

Cooper stood in front of Noah. *So why don't you just leave, and we'll act like this never happened? Or you could tell her you see me! This doesn't have to get complicated, pal.*

Noah chuckled. "I get that a lot. You sounded upset. Is there anything I can help with before I go into town?"

Sage waved a hand at him. "Oh, it's silly. I was just giving myself a little pep talk. Sometimes I get to thinking about how much work it is running an inn alone and get a little overwhelmed. But I'm okay now. How's the roof?"

Tell her she's not alone. Tell her I'm here, Cooper pleaded. *She needs me. We aren't like those other people you were talking about. A message from me will only make her stronger.*

"Six, maybe seven spots need to be replaced before the storm, but we'll need to replace the entire section over this area." He pointed to the dining room.

"Oh, we'll just put umbrellas over the tables, and then we won't have to worry about it. It'll give the dining room ambience," Sage said, opening a box on the floor. "Outdoor eating, indoors. We'll start a new trend. It'll be all the rage."

You have to tell her I'm here.

Noah shook his head.

"I'm kidding." She smiled at him. It was going to take a while for him to get used to her unusual sense of humor. "Get what you need at the hardware store. I already have an account there. But before you go, would you look at this sink? It turned into a geyser yesterday, and I'd really like to have it working today, if possible. I had my friend, Richard, look at it, but he's useless with a wrench."

Noah nodded and made his way to the sink.

Please, she is the love of my life. You have to reassure her that she's not alone. That I never left her, Cooper begged. *She has to know.*

Sage watched Noah study the faucet.

"You aren't really gonna sleep in the barn tonight, are you?" she asked

"That's the plan," said Noah, as he opened the cabinets beneath the kitchen sink.

"What about the dog?" asked Sage.

"Well, she'll either get used to me . . ." He fiddled with the pipes. ". . . or maul me to death."

Let's hope for the latter. Cooper said with a gruff voice. *Then I can give you that punch to the face you deserve for ignoring me and not telling Sage I'm here.*

Now, it was Sage's turn to stare at Noah. He looked over his shoulder from under the sink.

"I'm joking. We'll work something out." He stood and brushed his hands off. "All you need is a new faucet. The old one was just too worn to handle the surge of water pressure after being off for so long. Are you planning on replacing the entire sink?"

Cooper folded his arms. *She needs to replace you.*

Sage nodded. "I want to redo this entire kitchen. If it's gonna be open to the public, it needs to be totally redone."

"Then I'll just pick up a used faucet while I'm in town to get us by until we start on the kitchen."

"Okay," said Sage, "need me to go with you?"

Noah shook his head. "Not unless you need to go to town."

Or you're afraid he'll skip town. Which in my opinion is not a problem. We were fine without him before, we'll be fine again.

"Not really," said Sage. "I'll just stay here and unpack."

Heading toward the door, Sage went back to her box.

"You're not alone."

Cooper flung his hands in the air. *Finally, you've come to your senses and decided to tell her I'm here.*

"Huh?" Sage asked raising an eyebrow at Noah.

"I said, you're not alone. I'm here to help; you don't have to do this alone."

Having finished his list for the roof, Noah approached the barn. He had dealt with strays before, but if this one was too aggressive, he'd have no choice but to put her down. Knowing that wasn't what Sage wanted to do, he hoped he could just scare the mutt away.

Cooper appeared by his side.

"Go away," said Noah, "animals don't like ghosts."

So there's a greater chance of you getting eaten if I stick around? I think I'll stay.

Noah rolled his eyes. Most ghosts he could ignore, but Cooper was mouthy and was going to be a challenge. He'd really have to watch himself around Sage. All it would take would be one overheard conversation with Cooper, and Sage would either throw him out or use him as her personal walkie-talkie.

Slowly opening the barn door, Noah could make out the dog sitting in the corner. At first she just looked at him, her head cocked to the side. Then Cooper stepped in. She jumped up and arched her back, her teeth bared in a low growl.

"Get out," Noah muttered through clenched teeth. "You're scaring her."

Cooper smirked before running right at the dog, causing her to charge Noah.

Noah slammed the barn door tight, causing the dog to scratch and bark at the door. Latching it, he turned to Cooper who was laughing. "Oh, you think that's funny, huh?"

Cooper nodded unable to talk while laughing.

"I guess I'll be sleeping in the house."

Cooper stopped laughing. *You wouldn't dare.*

"You haven't left me much of a choice, have you?" Noah started to the house and chuckled. "Bet it's not funny now."

Chapter 8

Sage listened to the pounding on the roof. In the past week, hammering had become the soundtrack of her life. Noah had patched the roof, fixed the swing, and worked on the porch railing. The minute the supplies came in for the rest of the roof, he'd immediately started replacing the entire section over the dining room.

He was doing a fantastic job. After changing his mind about sleeping in the barn, they had gone from room to room, discussing the items that needed fixed and improvements Sage wanted to make. After that, they just kind of settled into a routine.

Sage would cook a big breakfast that they'd eat as they discussed the day's tasks. After breakfast, she'd clean up, all the scraps going to the dog, and Noah would gather supplies. Then they'd work on a project together. They might have three months before guests arrived, but there was no way she was leaving it all on Noah's shoulders. It was always going to be a team effort. She had just always thought she'd be helping Cooper with the renovation, not Noah.

She shook the thought away. The dishes washed, she laced up her boots and took a plate of scrambled eggs, complete with bacon, out to the dog.

You've got to stop feeding that animal, said Cooper. *It's never gonna leave.*

A chill rushed over Sage as she stepped outside causing her to turn her collar up. The wind was gusting, and there looked to be a storm just over the mountain. She glanced up at Noah on the roof resealing the chimney. There was no way that was safe.

"Noah," she yelled, "you better come down."

"Almost done," he hollered back as flurries whipped around her head.

"Okay, be careful. There's a storm rolling in. You've got ten minutes then I'm dragging you off that roof."

Or better yet, I could give him a nice shove.

Sage let out a whistle as she approached the barn. "Hey, puppy, I've got your breakfast. Better eat it fast."

This time the dog didn't wait for her to get back to the porch before gobbling up the meal. "I guess you were hungry," Sage said picking up the plate after the dog had returned to the barn.

Sage heard Noah cry out before hearing the dreadful thud of his body hitting the ground. Dropping the plate, she ran to him. "Noah, are you okay? Are you hurt?"

Cooper sneered. *We can only hope.*

"I'm fine." Noah rolled over onto his back and sat up, a grimace smeared across his face.

"No, you're not," said Sage, "I saw that look. Come on, let's get you inside."

The snow was coming down in big flakes. Sage looked to the north and didn't like what she saw. She'd lived in Wyoming long enough to know there was a blizzard coming.

Helping Noah inside, she eased him into her oversized chair. "Take off your shirt."

"I'm fine," Noah protested. "I need to get the tools off the roof before the snow sticks."

Sage, listen to the man. Everybody can keep their clothes on. Cooper looked at Noah. *Especially you.*

Placing her hands on her hips, Sage cocked her hip to the side. "Noah Finnley, quit being such a macho man. The tools are fine right now. My guess is you have a cracked rib from falling off the roof."

"I didn't fall off the roof," said Noah. "The ladder fell as I was coming down. I must not have gotten it locked into place, and it couldn't hold up to the wind gusts. It was a stupid mistake."

I'll say. Cooper laughed.

"Well, don't make another one by not letting me look at it. Now take off your shirt," Sage demanded once again. "I'm going to go get some Ace bandage strips to wrap your ribs up. I'm not taking any chances."

Sage walked to the supply closet and grabbed the first aid kit, along with some candles and a flashlight. When she returned, Noah sat shirtless trying to examine his own ribs. Sage sucked in a breath. This was the first time she had seen Noah without his shirt, his physique took her breath away.

Cooper reached out and slapped the flashlight causing it to tumble out of her hands. *Snap out of it. You're drooling.*

Noah turned as the flashlight hit the floor. "You dropped something." An ornery smile on his lips.

Crap, I forgot the slug could hear me.

"I, uh . . . yeah, I guess my hands are too full," stammered Sage. She cleared her throat. "Let's get those ribs wrapped up."

Noah held out his hand. "I can do it."

Sage raised an eyebrow. "Are you sure? It's gotta be tight."

I'll tighten it up for you, pal. Please let me do it.

Noah nodded. "Yeah, this isn't my first rodeo. I've had to do this a number of times on myself."

She handed over the bandages. "Okay, I'm gonna go get the tools, then light these candles and start a fire in case the electricity goes out. Let me know if you need any help."

A quick ten minutes later she hurried back inside. "This storm is gonna be a doozy. The tools and ladder are in just inside the barn. I also made sure the dog had some extra food and water. Not sure we'll be able to make it to the barn tomorrow."

Noah was making a second attempt on wrapping his ribs. "Are you sure you don't want my help?"

"I'll manage," he said.

She set the candles on the mantle, then bent to start the fire. Her back turned toward Noah, she forced herself not to turn around again until his shirt was back on. What was she thinking, staring at him like that? And what if he had caught her? She felt her cheeks glow red at the thought.

Fire started, she grabbed the candles and placed them around the room, then headed to the kitchen.

Ahhh, baby let me guess, you're gonna make some chili. One of my favorite parts of getting caught in a storm with you. He leaned into her. *Of course, not my favorite thing. Remember all those late stormy nights when I used to....*

Noah let out a loud cough then grabbed his ribs in pain, causing Sage to jump.

"Sorry," he said, pulling off the bandage, "there was something caught in my throat."

She turned to see Noah start on his third attempt.

"Please, let me help," she pleaded.

Noah sighed and handed Sage the bandage. "Fine, guess I'm out of practice. I thought I had grown out of being clumsy."

Unbelievable, said Cooper, *You'll do anything to get her arms wrapped around you.*

Sage quickly rerolled the bandage and started the tight wrap around Noah's chiseled abs. Every time her fingers touched his bronze skin, lightning shot up her body. As she leaned in close, she took in his scent, a mix of sawdust and soap, which seemed to make her head spin. Tucking the bandage in place, she quickly jumped up.

"I'm going to start a big pot of chili," she said. "It'll be something we can keep warm by the fire if we lose power. I cannot wait for my gas stovetop."

"Are you always this prepared?" asked Noah, easing his way up to join her in the kitchen.

Sage laughed. "One of my many quirks. Any time there's a big storm rolling in, I break out the candles and make a big pot of something like stew, soup, chili, or whatever I have on hand. I just know the one time I don't do all this prep work will be the time we get stuck in the dark without anything to eat. And trust me, you don't want to see this girl hungry."

Take her word for it, pal. She gets gruuumpy.

"Okay," said Noah, "at least let me help."

"Nonsense," said Sage, flipping a towel at him, "you just fell off the roof. You should rest."

"Correction, I fell off the ladder, and I'm fine." He sighed. "Besides I can't sit still. That's one of my many quirks."

Those quirks better not involve Sage later, you jackass.

"Are you sure?" Sage could feel her face soften. "What kind of creep makes someone work after they've fallen off the roof? "You really should take it easy."

Noah grabbed an onion out of the countertop basket. "Yes, now do you want this chopped or minced?"

The electricity went out just as the chili was ready. Noah and Sage sat on the floor in front of the fireplace, enjoying the warmth of both the food and the fire.

"Tell me a little bit about yourself, Noah Finnley." Sage scooted her empty bowl onto the coffee table beside her and leaned against the stone fireplace, enjoying its warmth.

Ugh, can't we just sit here in silence, whined Cooper, looking at Sage. *You were never one to let a moment of silence go by unnoticed.*

"There really isn't anything to tell. I already told you most of it," said Noah, scraping the last of his chili out of the bowl.

Oh, except for the part where you see her dead boyfriend and won't relay any messages. Yep, you left that part out, pal.

"No," said Sage. "You told me your job history. I want to know about you."

Placing his spoon in the now empty bowl, Noah set it next to Sage's bowl on the table and gently leaned back against the arm of the sofa, grimacing a bit with all the movement. "Well, let's see. Father died when I was young. Grew up with my mother and sister over in Sap Springs. End of story."

Why don't you just tell her the rest? Cooper bent in front of Noah. *There's a blizzard outside. It's not like she can run away or kick you out.*

Noah stretched out, sending his legs right through Cooper, ignoring the pain in his side.

Go ahead, ignore me. Cooper moved closer to Sage. *But I'm not going anywhere.*

"I'm sorry to hear about your father." Sage cocked her head to one side and gave him a sympathetic look.

"Oh, Sage, don't look at me like that. My father has been gone a long time."

Sage's hands flew up to her mouth. "I did not just do that. Tell me I did not give you the sympathetic stare? The 'bless your heart' look."

Noah laughed and then winced. "Afraid so, but I've never heard it called the 'bless your heart' look."

"After Cooper died, I had so many people coming up to me, giving me the sympathetic stare, while patting my hand or shoulder and saying, "Bless your heart." It got to the point where I just wanted to punch every well-wisher in the face, even though they were just trying to comfort me, but I felt they were being condescending somehow."

"And don't forget about the clichés," Noah added. His face grew serious as he patted Sage's hand. "Everything happens for a reason. You know, 'what doesn't kill you makes you stronger'."

Sage matched her face to his and placed her other hand on top of his. "He's in a better place."

Cooper let out a rush of breath as he watched Noah and Sage holding each other's hands. *Well, that's a load of crap.*

At that, Noah broke into a big belly laugh, holding his ribs and grimacing with each breath. Sage couldn't help but join him. Unlocking hands, they both sat back, clutching their sides as Sage let out a snort that sent them both back into hysterics.

"Stop making me laugh," said Noah, "My ribs can't take it."

Sage fanned herself. "It really isn't that funny. I don't know why I'm laughing like a loon."

"Must be something you put in the chili," said Noah, inspecting his bowl. "What about you?"

Sage raised an eyebrow. "What about me?"

"Where's your family? How'd you grow up?" asked Noah.

"Grew up here," she said. "Working class family. We made ends meet, but barely. I always knew we were poor, but I never felt like it, if that makes any sense. Both of my parents worked full-time jobs. I met Coop in middle school. He was such a pain in my butt. Always teasing me about one thing or another. His mother was pretty bad off. I don't know the whole story, but she became addicted to painkillers after an incident with Cooper's father put her in the hospital. So Coop spent a lot of time at my house. My parents treated him like family. When they died in a car accident about five years ago, Coop was the only family I had left." She looked into the fire. "Now it's just me, I guess."

I'm still your family, baby. Cooper placed his hand through Sage's hand that rested on the floor. It was the closest thing to holding it he could do.

"It's okay to miss him," said Noah.

"I know," Sage said, softly, "but it's such a buzz kill. How about a game of Monopoly? Looks like we're gonna be stuck in here for a while."

Don't let her be the top hat, Cooper cried out. *She always wins when she's the top hat.*

"Sure." Noah nodded. "But only if you let me be the top hat."

Chapter 9

The phone rang bringing Sage out of her wallpaper stripping trance. The good ol' 1975 yellow and green floral wallpaper did not want to come down. It had now become a war between Sage and the hideous flowers staring at her from the den. Sighing, she grabbed the receiver and looked at the caller ID expecting it to be Richard checking in on her yet again. He'd called four times since the storm hit. Sage began to wish the phone lines were still down.

But it wasn't him.

Raising an eyebrow, she answered the mystery call. "Hello?"

"Is this Sage McKennan?" a nasally voice asked from the other end.

"It is."

"Thank God. I've been trying to track you down for the past week," said the voice.

"Who is this?" asked Sage. "And how did you get this number?"

"Oh, sorry," said the voice. "My name is Ellen Criter. I run the Pleasant Valley Nursing home in Sap Springs. I got your number from the deputy's office. I called everywhere I could think of and finally reached a nice man by the name of Deputy Park who passed on your number."

"Oh, he did?" Sage crushed the strip of wallpaper she held in her hand. She wasn't ready to take reservations. Richard knew that.

"To be fair, I did tell him I was a friend of yours from high school trying to get reacquainted," Ellen said.

"You've gone to a lot of trouble. What can I do for you, Ms. Criter?" asked Sage.

"It's about your father-in-law…"

"There must be some mistake," interrupted Sage. "I've never been married."

Sage heard the rustle of papers as Ellen cleared her throat. "Says right here on the insurance claim that you are the benefactor of one Cooper Davis's estate. Is that correct?"

"Yes," Sage said slowly.

"Are you aware that Mr. Davis's father, Lucas Redhawk, has been living at the Pleasant Valley Nursing home in Sap Springs for the past three years?" Ellen asked.

Redhawk, it had been a long time since Sage had heard that last name. Her mind drifted back to the image of a young Cooper Redhawk before he had changed his last name to Davis. That young boy was as rowdy as they came. Not a day went by that he didn't end up in the principal's office for one offense or another. Usually it had to do with putting garter snakes in the desk of their third grade teacher, Mrs. Edward.

"I'm sure you have the wrong person." Sage shook her head, bringing herself back to the conversation at hand. "Cooper's father died three years ago."

"I assure you, Ms. McKennan, Mr. Redhawk, is most certainly alive, but he won't be for long if he keeps spitting on the nurses. There is no way to put this delicately; Mr. Redhawk can no longer stay with us. As far as I can tell, you are the closest thing he has to a relative. So it's your choice."

"You've lost me," Sage rubbed her forehead. "What's my choice?"

"You can either come get Mr. Redhawk, or he'll be sent to an adult care facility that specializes in state aid. He cannot stay here. Our state aid rooms are full."

Sage looked around Winter Song. There was more than enough room, but did she really want to take in a man she'd never met? And did Ms. Criter say that he spit on the nurses? Of course, what could she expect from a man who was the sole reason for Cooper's mother to be addicted to painkillers? She prepared herself to tell Mrs. Criter that she didn't care what happened to Lucas Redhawk, but the words stuck in her throat.

Pressure began building behind Sage's eyes as she remembered visiting her grandma in a state run nursing home. The visions of lonely senior citizens staring into space along paint-chipped hallways still gave her nightmares.

She saw her sweet grandma lying in that plain small room with nothing but the contents of her nightstand to call her own. Sage remembered her Grandma's sad smile the last time they left the depressing eggshell color room. Though she was only five, she wanted nothing more than to save her grandma from the place that seemed to breathe sadness. Her grandma died less than a month later, alone in that dismal room.

"Why is he in the nursing home?" asked Sage. "Can he not care for himself?"

"Mr. Redhawk is confined to a wheelchair, but he is not in need of medical attention. I'm sorry I can't tell you more unless you are his legal guardian, and you haven't signed those papers yet."

"So he doesn't need a nurse or a hospital close by? I live in the mountains. I'm not sure I can take care of him," said Sage. "I've never done anything like that before, and I'm just starting a business..."

"Ms. McKennan, I can tell this is all a shock." Ellen stated, interrupting Sage's train of thought. "All I can really say is that you don't need any special training to take care of Mr. Redhawk. I hate to be blunt, but I need an answer."

Visions of Sage's grandmother floated by again. She couldn't do it. She couldn't let Cooper's father rot in some unknown adult facility, no matter what had happened in the past or how much care he might need.

"He can stay with me," Sage answered.

"Oh, good," said Ellen. "I'll expect you tomorrow."

"Tomorrow?"

"Yes, as I said before, Mr. Redhawk's stay is up. We should've shipped him to another facility a week ago. We've been quite generous given the situation. He really is very nasty to our hard-working staff. You'll have your work cut out for you."

Sage glanced around the half-finished den. "You have no idea," she muttered.

"What was that Ms. McKennan?" asked Ellen.

"Nothing," said Sage, looking at her watch. "I'll be there by noon tomorrow."

"We'll see you then."

Sage slumped down into a deep brown armchair, phone still in her hand, as Cooper appeared by her side.

He looked at Sage and his face softened. *What is it, baby? What's wrong?*

Sage took in a deep breath. "What am I going to do with your father, Cooper? Why in the world did you tell me he was dead? Why would you lie about something like that?"

My father? Cooper's eyes narrowed. *Leave that bastard to rot. You don't owe him anything. He'll just ruin your life.*

Sage sighed again and pushed herself out of the deep chair. "Guess I better tell Noah that he's on his own 'till I get back."

As Sage exited the back door, Cooper rushed to Noah who was re-patching the roof. *I need you to tell her one thing.*

"I already told you 'no'," Noah mumbled as he heard the back door open and close.

Listen, she's about to tell you she's headed to Sap Springs to pick up my good-for-nothing father and bring him here. I told her he was dead for a reason. He's a mean bastard, and she needs to have nothing to do with him. She owes him nothing. He can rot in a gutter for all I care.

"She's a big girl. She can decide for herself," said Noah.

You don't understand, pleaded Cooper. *That man beat my mother and then left without a trace when I was nine years old. I sat with my mom for days in the hospital while they mended her broken bones. Those wounds sent her right into an addiction of pain killers and alcohol. She wouldn't even press charges against the S.O.B.*

"Hey, Noah," Sage hollered from the ground.

"Yeah," Noah hollered back still looking at Cooper.

"I have to go to Sap Springs." Sage paused, and Noah knew she was waiting for some kind of response. "Noah?"

"Yeah," he said again.

"Can you please come down? I need to know you're hearing me, and I don't want you to fall again."

Noah rubbed his jaw.

"Hold on," he hollered down and then looked at Cooper. "Let me talk to her, and then I want to know the whole story."

Noah walked to the edge and peered down at Sage. "You said you needed to go to Sap Springs?"

Sage held her hands over her eyes to block the sun that had finally decided to melt the blizzard snow. "Yes, I have to pick up Cooper's father. He's been staying at a nursing home, but he can't stay there anymore. So you're on your own for a couple of days. Are you okay with that?"

Noah nodded, glanced sideways at Cooper and then took a deep breath. "I know it's none of my business, but there are places that will take him in. You've already taken on a lot with this place. Are you sure this is what Cooper would want?"

Though her eyes were partly covered, Noah could see them narrow. "You're right. It isn't any of your business.

Cooper was my family, which means his dad is my family. I don't let family members rot in nursing homes."

Noah held up his hands. "Okay, I didn't mean to offend, just playing devil's advocate." He glanced again at Cooper.

Sage dropped her arms to her sides. "I'm sorry, Noah, I didn't mean to snap. It's a sensitive subject for me. I'm going to go pack."

Noah gave her a quick nod, and Sage made her way back inside.

You can't let her go get him, yelled Cooper. *He's dangerous! Why do you think I paid for him to stay at a nursing home on the other side of the state? I don't want Sage anywhere near him.*

"If he's so bad, then why did you put him in a nursing home at all?" asked Noah.

Cooper chewed on his lower lip. *It was my mother's dying wish. She never stopped loving the jerk. Right before she died, she found out he was in some kind of shoddy adult facility and couldn't stand the thought. So she asked me to move him some place nicer with the money she was leaving me. She left me just enough for a three year stay at Pleasant Valley. I gave them everything, and then left them with a fake contact number. I didn't expect to hear from him again. I never once thought they would call Sage and drag her into this whole mess.*

Cooper took in a deep breath. *The money my mom left me was enough for the down payment on this place. Putting him in that home was the sole reason I had to get on a cod boat to begin with. Had she not asked me to do that for him,*

Sage and I would've had this place three years ago. He's not just the reason my mom is dead. He's the reason I'm dead.

Noah took the story in, and then sighed as he turned to go down the ladder.

What are you going to do? asked Cooper. *Are you going to tell Sage you can see me so she won't go?*

"Nope," said Noah, making his way down the ladder. "I'm gonna go pack."

Chapter 10

Sage shifted the overnight bag to her right shoulder and made her way to her jeep. She was surprised to see Noah leaning against the hood. He had traded in his heavy Carhartt overalls for the more casual look of a grey sweater, loose fitting dark blue jeans, and a pair of brown loafers.

"You look nice. But those shoes are a little risky for working on the roof, don't you think?" Sage said, raising an eyebrow.

We can only hope he falls again, said Cooper. *Maybe it'll knock some sense into him, and then he'll relay my messages so you won't waste a trip to pick up my good-for-nothing father.*

"I'm going with you," Noah said, picking at the dirt under his fingernail.

Cooper stood in front of Noah. *That's not part of the plan, pal. You're supposed to stop her, not help her.*

Sage opened the driver's side door and tossed her bag on the back seat. "There's no need. I've got it handled."

"I'm sure you do," said Noah. "My sister still lives in Sap Springs, and I thought since you were going maybe I could tag along. I called her, and she did say we could stay with her and the twins tonight, which will save you a hotel room."

Ahhh... yes let's make this a family vacation. It's not like we have anything better to do, you know, like stop Sage from making the biggest mistake of her life. Even bigger than hiring you. Cooper turned in a circle kicking at the mud. *You have to stop her! Disconnect the battery, pull the fuel pump fuse, pour sugar in the gas tank. I don't care what you do, just don't let her bring that man back here.*

Sage hesitated. She was still reeling over the news of Cooper's dad and wanted time to mull it over, not spend the road trip trying to think of conversation starters.

"Unless you've changed your mind about picking up Cooper's father?" Noah stood tall.

Please say you've changed your mind, Cooper begged.

Sage shook her head. "I told you, he's family. I can't leave him there."

"Then I'll help you pay for the gas," Noah said holding up a cooler. "I make a mean peanut butter and jelly." He gave the cooler a little shake.

"You don't have any money," Sage teased, relenting a little while trying to mask her smile. "What kind of jelly?"

"Strawberry-Rhubarb."

"Why that's my favorite. How did you ever know?" Sage asked sarcastically.

"Well, since the blizzard, you don't have much in the fridge, besides eggs, and I didn't think they'd travel well."

She rolled her eyes.

Stop talking food and make her stay here, demanded Cooper. *He will ruin her life. Is that worth a vacation with your sister? You selfish good-for-nothing . . .*

Noah sighed. "Sage, I know how this looks. I haven't been working for you very long and now I'm trying to hitch a ride to see my sister instead of working . . ."

"And you raided my fridge." Sage winked.

"Hey now, that was part of the deal, room and board, remember?" Noah sat the cooler down on the hood of the jeep. "Look, I don't feel comfortable fixing your house while you're not here. There might be some tough decisions to make, and I'm not making them without your input. Second, I don't like the thought of you traveling all the way to Sap Springs to pick up a man you don't know by yourself. Cooper's father or not, you need someone in your corner. Third, and most important, my nieces are playing basketball tonight, and if we leave right now we can make most of the game. Their dad is a no-good rat, and they need to know someone is in their corner, too."

Cooper threw his hands in the air. *Now, she's definitely going to go. You just had to play the kid card. I knew this had nothing to do with her and everything to do with you.*

Sage looked at the ground.

"If I'm not riding with you," said Noah, "then I'm following you. I'm not going to let you face Cooper's father alone."

You shouldn't let her face him at all!

"What about the roof?" Sage asked.

"It's finished. It didn't lack that much when I started this morning," Noah answered. "We were lucky the blizzard didn't do any more damage. So technically, we're between projects, and it's the perfect time for a short break."

Sage sighed and climbed into the jeep. Leaning over, she opened the passenger side door. "Well, I thought you were coming."

Great, let's just have one big happy road trip, said Cooper before appearing in the front seat of the jeep. *You're sitting in back, pal.*

"Have it your way," Noah mumbled before sliding into the front seat, sitting directly on Cooper.

Not funny, pal. Cooper appeared in the backseat. *Don't you have any respect for personal space?*

"Thanks, Sage." Noah placed his hand on her arm, causing her to look up at him. "I really mean it. I haven't seen my nieces in a long time. I appreciate the ride."

Cooper kicked the back of Noah's seat causing him to jolt forward. *Hands off, pal.*

"You okay?" asked Sage.

"Yeah," said Noah, rubbing his neck. "I guess the seat wasn't locked in place."

Sage raised an eyebrow. "Ooookay . . ."

Sage glanced at the man sleeping with his head against the window. His tawny hair was cut short above his ears but left a little long on top, giving him a constant disheveled look. His tan, muscular arms crossed against his chest moved to the gentle rhythm of his breath. He reminded her of a Lost Boy following Peter Pan. Her mind fluttered back to the day he'd fallen off the ladder and had to take off his shirt. He was definitely not a boy.

I wish there was a way for you to hear me, Cooper said, leaning into Sage's ear. *Once my father is in your life, there's no way for me to protect you from him. Please feel me here. Please, baby, turn around and go back to Winter Song. I would never ask you to take care of him. I love you too much to put that on you.* He blew softly on the back of her neck.

Sage rubbed away the chill bumps that took over her neck without warning. "I hope I'm doing the right thing by you, Coop," she said softly. "I just wish I knew why you said he was dead."

Because he is to me. Cooper leaned back and crossed his arms. *I never wanted him in my life, and I definitely don't want him in yours.*

She glanced at Noah and was relieved to see he was still asleep and hadn't heard her talking to her dead boyfriend.

Shaking the thought away, Sage reached behind her to find the ice chest and managed to grab one of the peanut butter and jelly sandwiches without running off the road. Her mouth watered as she carefully unwrapped the makeshift lunch. Her breakfast seemed like ages ago. Taking a huge bite of the sweet concoction, she nearly choked.

Sage! Are you ok? Cooper bounced up and tried to pat her back, his hand going right through her.

Coughing, she pulled over the jeep, before spilling out the door and spitting out the rest of the sandwich. She fumbled in the ice chest looking for a bottle of water.

Cooper looked over at Noah, still snoring by the window. He kicked the back of Noah's seat before leaning forward and yelling in Noah's ear. *Wake up you idiot. Sage is in trouble!*

"What's going on?" Noah bolted up, looking around to catch his bearings. "Are we there?"

Sage finished chugging the water bottle. "What are you trying to do? Kill me?"

Noah rubbed his eyes and then looked at his watch. "Not real sure what you're talking about since I've been asleep for the past hour."

"That sandwich." Sage's eyes watered. "Did you make it for Satan?"

"Still not following," said Noah, rubbing the back of his neck and then looking at Cooper, who shook his head.

"Then you take a bite." Sage threw the sandwich at him.

Noah shrugged and took a huge bite of the offending PB&J. He chewed twice and his eyes grew wide. Opening the door, he spit the sandwich to the ground. Sage handed him a bottle of water.

Taking a huge gulp, he swished his mouth then spit it on the ground next to the sandwich. "I don't understand," he said. "That's the hottest cinnamon I've ever tasted. Is it foreign?"

"Cinnamon?" said Sage. "I'm out of cinnamon. Where did you find this so-called cinnamon? And who would put cinnamon on a peanut butter and jelly sandwich?"

"It was in the spice rack, with a big black C marked on it," said Noah. "It's my special ingredient."

"Well, it's special alright." Sage started laughing. "That was cayenne, you goof. Can't you tell the difference?"

Noah shook his head as he swished his mouth out again. "Hey, I'm not the one who leaves lethal weapons of mass destruction unmarked in the spice cabinet. Cayenne never even crossed my mind." He joined in the laughter. Soon both were snorting between gulps of water.

With a big sigh, Noah threw his empty water bottle in the backseat of the jeep. "Why don't you let me drive for a while?"

"Okay," said Sage, walking around to the passenger side. "It really is the least you can do after trying to poison me."

Noah slid behind the driver's seat. "I still say I was set up. You just thought I'd put it in my oatmeal, instead of our peanut butter and jellies."

"I plead the fifth," said Sage, as Noah pulled back onto the road.

"I hate to ruin the mood," said Noah, "but I have to ask why it's so important for you to pick up Cooper's father? And don't say because he's family again. We both know you've never met the man, and I can't help but think there's a good reason Cooper told you he was dead."

Finally! sang Cooper. *You're going to talk her out of this mess.*

Sage sighed. "When I was little, I went to visit my grandma in a nursing home. It was so sad and depressing, that I had nightmares. I can't leave Coop's dad to die like that."

He deserves worse.

"How do you know he won't get sent to a nice facility that has rooms available? With state aide, he could be sent to a number of places, some really nice," said Noah.

"I know it sounds silly." Sage leaned her head against the window, "but regardless of Coop's motives for telling me his father was dead, this man is the last earthly connection I have to Cooper. I guess I just want to hold onto him anyway I can."

Ahhh... baby, you don't have to use my father. You can hold onto me now, if only this jack wagon would tell you I'm here. Cooper glared at Noah.

Noah reached over and patted Sage's hand while giving her the sympathy look they'd discussed during the blizzard. "It's okay," said Noah. "Cooper is in a better place. Everything happens for a reason."

Sage stared at Noah, eyes wide. He smirked. Then they both starting laughing.

Cooper sat in the back and watched Noah and Sage have their laughing fit. He thought about kicking the back of Noah's chair again, but figured they'd just laugh harder. As good as it was to see Sage laugh again, his blood boiled that he wasn't the one making her so happy. He glared at Noah. He would find a way to make Noah relay his messages to Sage, and then Mr. Noah Finnley would be a ghost of a memory.

Chapter 11

Noah rubbed his jaw as he waited for his sister to answer the door. She was not going to be happy that he brought a ghost to her doorstep, but maybe Becca could help him convince Cooper to go into the light. Then again, she might tell Sage everything.

Becca never was one to hide from her gift, but she didn't embrace it either. Now that she had her girls, she didn't want ghosts anywhere near her. As far as they could tell, the ten-year-old girls did not share their mother's ability.

As the door creaked open, Noah forced a smile. "Becca!"

Becca yanked open the door and slammed into her brother with a big bear hug. "Baby brother! You made it just in time. I was just headed to Katie and Kellie's game." She looked at Sage, and Noah cringed when Becca locked eyes with Cooper.

"I'd like you to meet my friend, Sage," Noah interjected before Becca could mention Cooper. "As I told you on the phone, I'm helping her fix up her B&B down in Beaverton."

Sage extended a hand. "Thanks for letting us stay, Becca. Hope you don't mind me tagging along to the game."

"It's not you I mind," Becca mumbled, raising an eyebrow before turning to Noah. "Well, come on in."

Sage walked through the door, followed closely by Noah, who closed the door behind him before Cooper could walk through it.

Ahhh, come on, Finnley. Cooper threw his hands up in the air. *That's just rude. You know I can get in other ways.*

Cooper tried to appear in the house, just as he'd done countless times at Winter Song, but didn't budge. Then he placed his hand on the wall, ready to walk through the structure. His hand sank in, but became stuck. He yanked it out of the tar-like substance. *What the . . . ?*

Noah opened the door and then looked over his shoulder to talk to Sage. "I'm gonna grab the bags, be right back."

As he exited the house, he motioned to Cooper to follow him.

I can't get in the house. What kind of trick are you playing, Finnley?

"It's not me." Noah pointed to the red wreath with berries and twigs on the door. "That wreath is made of Rowan and red twine."

I'm not here for the Home and Garden Show! I'm not gonna leave you in there alone with Sage. Tell me how to get inside, yelled Cooper.

"That's what I'm trying to tell you. Becca has the gift, too, and bought that wreath from an elder Celtic lady to make sure we always have a safe haven to go to. You are not allowed in the house."

Oh great, so are you going to do that at Winter Song so I can't enter my own house? Cooper bumped his chest against Noah's.

"Trust me, I would if I could, but I can't. It has to be the owner of the house. Sage would have to do it."

So you could just buy her a wreath and kick me out?

Noah shook his head. "No, she has to buy it for that particular purpose. If Becca didn't believe in the Rowan's power to keep spirits out, it would just be another door ornament." Noah grabbed the bags. "So you'll just have to stay in the jeep."

Like hell I will. Cooper puffed up his shoulders. *I'll make it through that sludge.*

"Wouldn't try it unless you want to be stuck for eternity." Noah shook his head. "Well, maybe not eternity, but until she takes the wreath down, and she'll die before she decides to do that."

Noah started toward the door. "I'd say I'm sorry, but I'm not. A night without you will be a vacation. Don't worry about Sage. I'll see to her. Oh, and don't try to jump in Becca's van either. She has Rowan hanging from her rearview mirror."

Noah laughed as Cooper let out a string of curses.

"What's so funny?" asked Sage as Noah entered the house.

"Ahh, just some moron being a jerk outside. He's gone now. Didn't like his sleeping arrangement for the evening. I told him he was talking to the wrong person." Noah winked at Becca.

"Noah, can I get you to look at the girl's toilet before we go to the game," Becca asked. "It just keeps running."

Noah gave Sage an apologetic look as he set down the bags. "Do you mind? I'll be right back."

Sage shrugged. "Go ahead."

"Make yourself at home," Becca said, gesturing to the living room. "I'm sure this will only take a minute. It's just been driving me crazy."

Becca grabbed Noah's hand and dragged him to the back bathroom.

"You brought a ghost to my house," she hissed. "How could you? You know how I feel about that. In fact, I thought we were on the same page when it came to that. You've got about a minute to explain before your pretty 'friend' starts to wonder what's up."

Noah held up his hands. "His name is Cooper, and he's refusing to go into the light. He wants me to relay messages to Sage. They have quite the history."

"His wife?"

Noah shook his head. "No, but they were together for a long time before he died."

"Well, then relay the message and send him on his way." Becca flushed the toilet.

"He's determined to stay with her forever." Noah rubbed his jaw. "Besides you know I don't do that, not since Mom."

"So you're just ignoring him?" Becca shook her head.

"That's the plan, hoping he'll get the point."

"Sounds foolish to me, but he's your problem." She turned to leave, then faced him again. "But don't you dare leave him here. He goes into the light or back to Beaverton. I mean it, Noah."

"I know you do, Sis. Trust me I wouldn't want to be the person responsible for haunting your house."

"You got that right. Now, let's get to that game." She pulled Noah out of the bathroom, and came face to face with Sage.

"Sorry," said Sage. "I just want to make sure it's okay that I'm here. I can still get a hotel, and Noah can stay and visit with you and your daughters."

"Actually . . . ," Becca started.

"Becca was just saying you could sleep in the girls' room now that the toilet is fixed, and they can have a slumber party in the living room. Weren't you, Becca?" Noah interjected, giving his sister a quick squeeze on the shoulder.

"No, that's not what I was saying at all." Becca elbowed her brother. "But it's actually a great idea. I was going to have you stay in my office on the futon, but Noah can sleep there. That mattress is crap anyway. Can't have a guest sleeping on it."

"Hey, I'm a guest," said Noah holding up his hands.

"No, brother dear, you're family, so you get to put up with the lumpy mattress. Lord knows I'm putting up with a lot more from you." Becca let out an awkward laugh. "Well, let's go. We can go in my van, plenty of room for all the warm bodies."

Sage slouched against the wicker chair in the pizza parlor and threw her napkin on her plate. "That was by far the best pizza I've ever eaten. You girls are gonna have to roll me out of here."

The twins giggled in unison. "So, Sage, are you single?" one of them asked. Sage was still having a hard time telling them apart, but she thought it might be Katie.

"Don't be rude, Kellie," chided Becca. So much for Sage's guess.

"It's okay. I used to be ten once, and I'm sure I asked the same embarrassing questions to my parents' houseguests." She nodded. "I am single."

"Did you have a boyfriend or a husband?" asked Katie.

Sage looked at her plate as she thought of Cooper. "Yes, I did," she said softly.

"Katie, do you have a boyfriend?" asked Noah. "Looked to me like that boy with the long hair was flirting. And Kellie, what's up with that red-headed boy? Really? A red-head? Do you want your future babies to have freckles?"

"Noah, don't even mention them having babies. They are way too young for that nonsense." Becca playfully slapped her brother on the arm.

"What happened to your boyfriend? Why are you single now?" asked Katie, seeming unfazed by her uncle's teasing.

"Seriously, that's enough, Katie," Becca's voice grew gruff. "It's none of your business."

"It's okay," said Sage. "I've only dated one man. His name was Cooper, and he died as a hero last year saving a young boy from drowning in the Bering Sea."

"What did he look like?" asked Kellie.

"Oh, he was very handsome. He had brown hair, long, but not too long. I guess you could call it shaggy, but in a good way. His eyes were as dark as two chocolate drops. I always told him that's why I fell in love with him, because his eyes reminded me of chocolate, and I love chocolate."

Katie looked at Kellie. "I told you so, Kellie. I knew he was with her."

Becca jumped up, knocking her chair over. "Well, it's time to go. Girls, come help me pay the check. I'll even let you play that stupid claw game."

The girls hopped up and ran to the claw machine, pointing out the stuffed animals they each wanted to grab.

"What did she mean?" asked Sage. "Did you tell them about Cooper?"

"Oh, you know how ten year olds are." Noah shrugged. "They change the subject every thirty seconds. They were probably talking about one of their friends."

"It didn't sound that way to me." Sage stood. "I'm gonna ask them."

Noah grabbed her arm. "Don't. I can explain."

Sage raised an eyebrow. "Go on."

Noah let go of Sage and rubbed his jaw. "My sister Googled you. I'm sure the girls saw Cooper's picture with the article but didn't really know the context."

"She Googled me?"

"Please, don't be mad. She's always looked out for me. When I told her I was going to work and live on your place, of course she was concerned. You know as well as I do that this arrangement is unusual."

Sage nodded. "I guess I should go talk to her. Let her know I understand, and I'm not a psycho."

Noah shook his head. "If I were you, I'd let it go. She's probably really embarrassed right now. Let me talk to her."

Sage started toward the door. "Okay, I need some air anyway. I'll be outside when you're ready to go."

Watching Sage leave, Noah approached his sister.

"Did you tell her?" asked Becca.

"Nope," said Noah, "she thinks you looked her up on the internet, and the girls saw Cooper's picture."

Becca shrugged. "Well, that's not completely untrue. I did look her up on the internet." She sighed. "I wonder where the girls saw him. And how long have they been able to see spirits? I can't believe they didn't tell me."

"Maybe they were afraid to bring it up," said Noah. "Maybe they thought you wouldn't believe them. It's not like you've told them you can see dead people. My guess is they saw Cooper at the basketball game. He knew we were going to one. It wouldn't have taken him long to find out which school," said Noah.

"Why didn't we see him?" asked Becca. "I saw other spirits there."

"Because he didn't want you to see him. He just wanted to keep an eye on Sage."

The girls giggled over.

"Are y'all talking about Sage's boyfriend?" Katie asked.

Becca nodded. "Where did you see him?"

"He was at the ballgame. Kept hiding in the corner," explained Kellie.

"We'd never seen him at the games before, and he kept staring at Uncle Noah," said Katie. "In fact, he's hiding behind the pinball machine right now."

Noah glanced over his shoulder just in time to see Cooper disappear. Probably went outside to be with Sage, he thought.

"How long have you two seen ghosts?" asked Becca. "You've never said anything about it."

"For as long as I can remember," said Katie. "For a long time we just thought everyone could see them."

"Have you told anyone?" asked Noah.

"Ummm... no," Kellie answered sarcastically. "We heard you and Mom talking about it one night and figured out that not everyone can see dead people. Hey, can we come out to your bed and breakfast sometime and talk to Cooper? He's hot."

"Absolutely not," said Becca. "And not a word to Sage, you hear me? There are rules, but we'll talk about those later."

Chapter 12

Sage pulled into a parking spot in front of the Pleasant Valley Nursing home and sighed.

"You sure you want to go in alone?" Noah asked.

Sage nodded. "I've never met Cooper's dad. The last thing I want is for him to get the wrong impression about you and think I didn't care for his son."

Like he's one to judge, Cooper said with a snort and then leaned into Noah. *Tell her to back this car up and leave the bastard. Or I'll start haunting your darling little nieces at school. I didn't want to go there, but you're leaving me little choice, Finnley.*

Noah's jaw tightened. "It's not too late to change your mind." Noah tried to sound casual. "No one would fault you for not taking in a man you've never met. I'm sure we can find some place affordable that's better than Statehaven. I don't think you've looked at all your options. You could be rushing this decision a bit."

Sage shook her head. "I told you, there's only one option. If he gets to be too much, I'll find a place for him closer to Winter Song." She smiled. "Aren't you supposed to keep him in line? Isn't that why I let you come along?"

Noah nodded as Sage got out of the jeep. "I don't know how long this will take. You should've stayed with your sister."

"I'll wait here," said Noah unbuckling his seatbelt and sticking his arm out the open window. "There's no reason for you to backtrack across town."

There's no way I'm sitting here while she makes a huge mistake, Cooper said.

"Wait," mumbled Noah, "I'll work on her to get your dad out of Winter Song, but no matter what, you leave my nieces out of this." He turned toward Cooper. "I mean it, Cooper; they're just kids."

Cooper raised his eyebrows and passed through the jeep to follow Sage inside.

The automatic doors slid open for Sage, and she took a deep breath to steady her nerves as she approached the reception area.

"Ellen Criter, please," she said to the young woman behind the desk.

An older woman with a pinched nose and short, straight grey hair came around the corner and handed the young woman a file. "I'm Mrs. Criter. How can I help you?"

"I'm Sage McKennan. I'm here to pick up Lucas Redhawk."

"Looks like I won the office pot," Mrs. Criter said to the young woman, smiling.

Sage raised an eyebrow.

Mrs. Criter waved her off. "We had a bet going. Most of the nurses thought you wouldn't show. But I knew better," she sang and held out her hand to the young woman, who handed her a stack of fives.

See Sage, said Cooper, *even the nurses know he's better left at some adult facility. Just tell her you've made a mistake, and they can send him anywhere but home with you. They'll understand. No one will think less of you. Please, baby, let's go.*

"Guess I should share half of this with you," said Mrs. Criter waving the stack of five dollar bills.

"That's really not necessary. Could we please get on with it? I'd like to meet Mr. Redhawk." Sage shifted her feet.

You'll get over that soon enough, said Cooper. *I mean at least take the money. It's not nearly enough, but it's something.*

Mrs. Criter smiled. "Of course, Ms. McKennan, right this way."

Sage cringed as they passed a lost looking woman taking baby steps. The tennis balls on the bottom of the walker making a sick squeak with every step.

"Good afternoon, Mrs. Lark. Off on a journey I see," Mrs. Criter chimed before grabbing her walkie-talkie. Pressing the button, she talked softly into the device. "Someone come see to Mrs. Lark. She's on the run again."

Sage's heart lurched as she looked over her shoulder at poor Mrs. Lark.

"She forgets where she is," Mrs. Criter said shaking her head. "Poor thing, her husband died a month ago, and she just keeps trying to go to the store to get his Tums. Here we are."

Mrs. Criter pointed to a heavy oak door covered in signs: "Watch for flying food," "Please do not leave patient unattended with bed pan," "Careful, patient bites!"

Sage swallowed hard.

"He can always go to another facility," said Mrs. Criter, her hand on the door knob. "He doesn't know you're coming. I don't have to tell him."

Listen to the lady, Sage, Cooper begged.

Sage shook her head. "No, he's family. I'll take him home."

Mrs. Criter chewed on the end of a pen. "Can I ask you a personal question before we go in?"

"If you're going to ask me why I'm taking him in, it's simple, he's family," said Sage, annoyed she had to keep repeating herself.

Mrs. Criter shook her head. "No, one of the reasons it took me so long to find you was because I kept looking for a Cooper Redhawk, not a Cooper Davis. I know it's none of my business, but why didn't he have the same last name as his father."

Because I didn't want to share a last name with a wife beater who runs from his mistakes instead of owning up to them. Cooper rolled his eyes. *Please, Sage, don't do this.*

Sage swallowed hard. Cooper never liked to talk about his father. "Cooper and his father had a falling out about a year before I met him. He never told me what happened exactly, but the minute he turned eighteen, he legally changed his last name to his mother's maiden name."

"I see," said Mrs. Criter, pushing the door open. "Mr. Redhawk, you have a visitor."

Sage entered the room and stared at the old man sitting in a wheelchair. His straight grey hair fell past his shoulders, and his face was locked in a constant stare at the plain beige wall. Sage walked to Cooper's father and knelt. Touching his hand very gently, she looked into his worn face.

"Mr. Redhawk, I'm Sage McKennan. I was your son's..." Sage looked down. She didn't know what to say. Girlfriend seemed so insignificant to what they had meant to each other, but they were never officially engaged, much less married. "Well, let's just say I loved him very much."

Sage looked at Mrs. Criter. "Does he know about Cooper?"

The man never gave a rat's ass about me before. I doubt he would now, Cooper said, crossing his arms.

Mrs. Criter gave a quick nod. "He's been told, not that he reacted to the news. But yes, he does know."

Cooper let out a loud laugh. *Told you he didn't care.*

Sage looked back at Mr. Redhawk. "I've decided you should come live with me. I hope you'll be happy at Winter Song. That's the bed and breakfast I own."

When he didn't reply, Sage glanced at Mrs. Criter. "Is he sick?"

Sick is an understatement, Sage. Cooper paced next to her. *Please, don't do this. He will make your life hell, just like he did my mom's. For the love of God, I wish that good for nothing carpenter would get off his ass.* Cooper kicked the wheelchair, causing it to roll slightly. Lucas Redhawk gripped the chair.

"I assure you there's nothing wrong with Mr. Redhawk," Mrs. Criter locked the wheelchair brake. "Other than his attitude. He's been seen by our best specialists, and they can't find any medical reason for him not speaking or walking." Mrs. Criter shrugged. "Most likely it's psychological, but since he won't interact with any of our counselors, we have no way of knowing if it can be cured or if he's just given up."

Giving up is what he does best. Cooper sneered at his father.

"Okay," said Sage, "let's get his stuff, shall we?"

A soft knock on the door was followed by Noah's head. "Sorry to interrupt. I'm here to help Ms. McKennan with Mr. Redhawk's things."

Sage glared at Noah. "Thought you were waiting in the car?"

"Just seeing if you need any help," Noah said, innocently.

Of course she needs help. Tell her to leave this piece of crap here, pleaded Cooper.

Noah grabbed a suitcase off the bed. "Is there anything else?"

"No," said Mrs. Criter. "He didn't have much to start with. You can keep the wheelchair. It was paid for by Mr. Davis."

And what about your nieces? Cooper crossed his arms. *Should I pay them a visit?*

Noah's jaw tightened again.

"Are you okay, Noah?" Sage asked.

"Fine," Noah replied.

"Alright," said Sage, releasing the brake and pushing Lucas toward the door. "Let's get you home."

As Sage finished the paperwork finalizing Lucas' departure from Pleasant Valley, Noah placed the luggage in the trunk. "Cooper," he whispered.

Cooper appeared by his side. *Come to your senses? Ready to put your nieces above this lying sack of crap that calls himself my father?*

Noah turned and punched Cooper hard in the gut. To Cooper's surprise, he felt the pain of the hit and stumbled backward.

What the . . . Cooper exclaimed right before Noah grabbed him by the neck.

"I've always believed in free will," growled Noah, "even for spirits. It's your choice about when you go into that light. But you're not the only one who can make things happen, and I swear if you go near my nieces, I will throw you into the light, and you'll never see Sage again. Do we understand each other?" The light appeared right behind them.

Cooper nodded, and the light faded as Noah let go.

Chapter 13

"I know it's not much," said Sage, wheeling Lucas into his new bedroom, "but it has an excellent view of the bird feeders." She pushed open the curtains, exposing six feeders attached to tall pines.

"We get a number of birds down here by the lake." Sage rambled on as she unpacked Lucas's suitcase. "This was going to be my office, but I can just as easily put a desk in my room. Noah's working on a ramp for the porch now, so you can go outside if you'd like. As soon as we get the place fixed up, we'll have boarders. There are three bedrooms upstairs so it'll be cozy, but hopefully you won't feel too crowded. Noah's taking one of the bedrooms up there now until he gets the barn fixed up."

Sage bit her lip. "You might be wondering about Noah and me--about our relationship. Well, I can assure you that we are just business partners. He needed a place to live, and I needed a carpenter. This place has good bones, but even good bones sometimes need a plastic surgeon."

She glanced at Lucas, who continued to stare out the window. "Anyway, I just wanted to let you know there's no romance going on there. Just in case you were wondering."

After hanging the last shirt, Sage bent and looked Lucas in the eyes. "I don't know if you can hear me, but I loved your son very much. I just wanted you to know that."

Standing back up, Sage brushed her hands on her jeans. "Well, you're all unpacked. I'll give you some peace and make us some dinner. I'm sure you're hungry after that long drive. I know I am."

Sage took one last glance at Lucas, hoping for a reaction. Getting none, she headed to the kitchen.

You know, said Cooper, *you could just wheel him out to the woods and let the elements take care of him. No one would ever know.*

Sage grabbed some eggs, ham, cheese, butter, and green onions from the fridge and began chopping the ham and onions.

I do miss your omelets, said Cooper, licking his lips. *I don't think you ever made a meal I didn't like, come to think of it. Except for that time you tried to make the Reuben sandwich casserole that was tangy enough to make a German pucker.* He laughed at the thought.

Finishing the first omelet, Sage slid it onto a paper plate.

Oh crap, you're gonna go feed that dog again aren't you? Cooper stepped in front of her, only to have her walk right through him. *This is a bad idea, Sage*, he said trailing after her. *It's bad enough you're feeding her that pricey dog food, you've got to stop giving her people food.*

Sage walked toward the barn and let out a low whistle. "Here puppy, puppy," she called, setting the plate a few feet from the door and backing up a few feet more.

Sage, don't, Cooper begged.

"What are you doing?" asked Noah, coming up behind Sage.

"Trying to make friends with the dog so you can have the barn, and I don't have to call animal control. Having a dog around is a good idea," said Sage. "But we can't wait much longer to get started on this barn."

It's not a good idea if the dog's feral! exclaimed Cooper. *Finnley, you can't think this is a good idea.*

"What if it's rabid?" asked Noah. "Not really a perk for the B&B."

"This dog is not rabid," Sage said matter-of-factly, "It could've taken me out the very first day I got here, but didn't. It's just not used to having company. Besides, a dog can keep mountain lions and bears off the property."

"And the deer, elk, rabbits, squirrels," said Noah.

Sage rolled her eyes. "I've seen plenty of wildlife around here, and I've never seen this dog chase so much as a ground squirrel. We've got all winter to tame her. The first step is getting her out of the barn. Now, shhh."

The dog peeked its head out of the barn door, nose raised in the air. It sniffed a couple of times and took a step towards the plate.

"That's it, puppy," Sage whispered. "Come on."

Sage get to the porch. You should've come out here with a pitch fork, Cooper complained, stepping toward the dog. *This dog is gonna attack you one day and then eat you for breakfast.*

The dog started growling, and Sage took a few more steps back. Cooper stepped in front of Sage, causing the dog to bark and bear its teeth.

"Come on," said Noah, urging Sage to the house. "I think she needs a little more time to get used to us." Sage backed slowly toward the porch.

"You too," Noah muttered to Cooper. "You're making it worse."

"What did you say?" asked Sage.

Noah shook his head. "Nothing, I was just saying I wouldn't want to share my omelet either. It sure smells good."

Sage smiled. "Well, let's get you one then." She turned and went inside the house.

"I'll be right there," Noah called after her. "Just gonna grab this plate so it doesn't blow away when she's done."

Noah turned to Cooper. "That dog isn't barking at Sage."

Are you blind? We both saw it. Cooper gestured toward the barn. *That mutt growled and then barked at her. It's only a matter of time before Sage gets bitten.*

"That's not what I saw at all," said Noah, rubbing his jaw. "The dog didn't start growling and barking until you took a step toward it. I think she can see you, and I don't think she likes what she sees."

Cooper laughed. *So let me get this straight, the only beings on this God forsaken planet that can see me are a washed up carpenter and his family, who won't relay my messages, and Cujo, the rabid barn dog?* Cooper shook his head. *I'm in Hell. This must be Hell.*

"I'm just telling you what I saw," said Noah. "You don't have to listen to me."

And just why should I listen to you? asked Cooper. *You didn't stop Sage from bringing my father here. You won't call animal control on the devil dog. You won't even relay a simple message for me. But you want me to listen to you?*

"There is only one thing I want you to do, and that's go into the light. We both know you aren't the listening kind." Noah grabbed the plate and walked toward the house.

Thanks a lot, pal, yelled Cooper after Noah. *At least I'm concerned for her safety, which is a lot more than I can say for you!*

Sage slid the plate in front of Noah. "I hope you like it." Picking up a tray of food, she started toward Lucas's room. "I'm going to try and get Lucas to eat."

Let him starve, Cooper said, appearing by her side. *The devil dog deserves the food more than he does. I know, feed him to the dog: Lucas will be eaten, and then the dog will probably die of food poisoning--win, win.*

Lucas was in the same position Sage had left him in just under an hour before. "I hope you like omelets," she said. "I haven't been to the grocery store yet this week, so it's slim pickings."

Setting the tray down on a small desk, she wheeled Lucas to it. "I thought you'd be more comfortable eating in here today, but usually we'll eat in the dining room or kitchen."

He's not comfortable unless he's sitting in front of the T.V. with a beer and a frozen dinner. Cooper laughed. *There's no need to go out of your way for him. He doesn't deserve your kindness.*

Before Sage had time to apply the wheelchair brake, Lucas grabbed the plate and threw it across the room. The plate bounced off the door frame and shattered.

Noah ran into the room, mouth full of eggs. "Everything okay?" he asked, raising an eyebrow.

Sage glared at Lucas. "I guess Mr. Redhawk isn't hungry."

I bet you wouldn't have done that if it'd been fried chicken and homemade noodles, you crazy old fool. Cooper grunted. *You're wasting your time, Sage. Let him starve to death.*

Sage grabbed the trash can and started throwing the plate shards and egg away. "Here's the deal, Lucas. I'm gonna bring you breakfast, lunch and dinner. You'll have two choices: one eat like a gentleman or two have me force feed you like a one year old." She closed the distance between them. "If you think for one second I'm going to let you starve yourself to death, you've got it all wrong, buddy. Like it or not, you and I are family and I don't let family kill themselves. I'll let you ponder that for a while."

Cooper sighed. *You better listen, old man. She will shove that food down your gullet.*

Sage carried the garbage can back to the kitchen. Slamming it down, she washed her hands.

"Can I make a suggestion?" Noah asked finishing his omelet.

Sage grabbed a towel and leaned against the counter. "I'll take all the suggestions I can get at this point."

"Forget breakfast tomorrow."

Sage opened her mouth to speak, and Noah held up a hand. "Hear me out, okay?"

Sage nodded.

"Make a big lunch instead. Something that will be too tempting to throw across the room." Noah tilted up his head. "Something like fried chicken and homemade noodles."

Cooper groaned. *You heard me say that, and now you're gonna take credit for knowing that old coot's favorite meal.*

Noah tilted his head. "It's a bit of a selfish request on my part. I do love some fried chicken."

Unbelievable. Cooper threw his hands in the air.

"That's not a bad idea." Sage started chopping ham for her own omelet. "And better yet, I'll make him eat it outside. That way if he throws it at least the dog can eat it."

"Speaking of the dog," Noah said, taking his plate to the sink and rinsing it. "What are your plans?"

Sage crossed her arms. "I don't think she's leaving me much of an option. I'll probably call Animal Control tomorrow. I really hate to do that. I know they'll just shoot her. It breaks my heart, but she's making it very hard to be her friend. It just seems unfair since she was here first. And I know if Coop were here, he'd make sure it never came to that. Makes me feel like I've let him down."

Cooper felt an ache in his chest. It would break Sage's heart to have the dog put down. He thought about what Noah said about the dog not liking him being around. Maybe the carpenter did have a point, this time.

Noah, said Cooper. *Ask her to give it a few days. I have an idea.*

"Why don't you give it a couple of days?" suggested Noah. "Think about it. We were here, then we were stuck inside due to the blizzard, and then we left. Give her some time to get used to us being around all the time. I think she'll come around."

"My, aren't you full of advice today?" Sage smiled.

"Just trying to live up to this 'being your partner' business. Thanks for the grub." He laid a hand briefly on her arm. "I'll be on the roof until dark putting the finishing touches on the chimney."

Sage felt the tingling sensation crawl up her arm. She watched Noah walk out the door. She hadn't had that sensation since Cooper. It had been almost a year. Maybe she should think about moving on.

The smell of burnt eggs assaulted her nose causing her to zap out of her trance. "Crap!" she yelled, pulling the omelet off the burner.

"Guess the dog will get two omelets today," she said.

Opening the windows, Sage caught a glimpse of Noah as he climbed onto the roof. Her heart skipped a beat.

"No," she whispered. "Do not go down this road with him. He is your carpenter and your employee at Winter Song. Nothing else. You're just friends. He's just like Richard."

But Richard Park had never sent lightning bolts up her arm. Sage shook the thought from her mind and concentrated on making another omelet.

Chapter 14

Cooper cursed as he walked toward the barn. Why in the world was he listening to Noah Finnley? The only thing that stray dog was good for was spreading fleas, and here he was on his way to make friends with the infested creature.

Taking a deep breath, Cooper walked through the barn door. He could just make out the dog sleeping on her side in the corner. She hadn't heard him come in. Cooper concentrated until his feet hovered over the dirt floor. If the dog was going to try to bite him, she was in for a surprise.

As he approached the sleeping animal, she opened an eye and let out a low growl.

Cooper held up his hands. *I come in peace,* he said, then laughed at himself. *This is ridiculous.*

Then he thought of Sage and regained his composure and lowered his feet to the floor. If he was going to make this work, he better make the dog see how normal he was.

The dog rolled over onto her belly and growled again.

Ok, look, I know you don't like me, Cooper started. *But you can't kill me. I'm already dead. I want us to be friends.*

Cooper reached toward the dog. She sprang to her feet and tried to bite Cooper's hand, her teeth hitting nothing but air. He was thankful that not all beings that could see him or touch him the way Noah did with the punch in the parking lot.

The dog let out a low growl with a hint of whining confusion.

See, I told you, Cooper said quietly. *You can't hurt me. But that's okay, because I don't want to hurt you either. I know I'm different. You're used to smelling "alive" humans. I bet I smell funny, if I smell at all.*

The dog cocked her head as Cooper sat down. Backing up, the dog let out another low whine, as her ears flattened.

It's okay. I'm just going to sit here and let you get used to me being around. I know it's weird, but you don't need to be afraid of me. I promise I won't hurt you. I want to be friends.

The dog continued to cower in the corner.

I'll sit here all day if I have to, said Cooper, his brown hair falling into his eyes. *I need you to like me so you'll like Sage. You know, the pretty girl who keeps feeding you?*

The dog sat, tail tucked beneath her legs and stared at Cooper.

"So what are you going to name her?" Noah asked Sage as she fried the chicken.

"Name who?"

"The dog."

Sage covered the skillet with a fry guard and looked at Noah. "Aren't we getting a little ahead of ourselves? You want me to name a dog Animal Control will probably have to come out here and shoot?"

"First off, I don't think it'll come to that." Noah stared at the ceiling checking for leaks as a sprinkler ran on the roof. "Second, if something has to be done about the dog, I'll take care of it. There's no need to have Animal Control come out. There'll be paperwork, and it'll be on record. Not good for tourism."

"You could do that?" Sage asked, then sighed. "I know I couldn't."

Noah shook his head. "I wouldn't want to, but if she has to be put down, it needs to be done right. I don't want some wannabe cop coming in here, guns a-blazing."

"Well, I hope you're right, and it doesn't come down to that." Sage stirred the noodles. "Do you have any names in mind?"

"Nothing specific, but it can't be frilly. No FiFi or Fluffy will work for that dog."

Sage rolled her eyes. "Like I would do that to the poor dog. You're right though, she needs a good strong name with meaning."

"How 'bout Rocky? You know for the Rocky Mountains." Noah stepped on a chair and examined the area around the light fixture for water.

Sage wrinkled her nose. "Pretty sure she'd bite me if I named her that. How about Xena?"

"As in the warrior princess?" Noah raised an eyebrow. "Kind of cheesy."

"It's not that cheesy. Lots of people name their male dogs Hercules."

"Not people who like their dogs."

"What about Athena?" Sage cut some more noodles and added them to the pot.

Noah wrinkled his nose. "How 'bout Barney? I mean she does live in the barn."

Sage laughed. "You're horrible at this. You can't just name an animal after where it sleeps. I have the perfect name, Alexandria, and we'll call her Lexi."

"Why Alexandria?" asked Noah, stepping off the chair and moving it to the far corner.

"Well, it means protector, and she is protecting the barn. Plus, it's pretty without being *frilly*."

"I like it," said Noah. Then he changed the subject. "Things seem to be going pretty well with Lucas."

"Aside from his refusal to eat?" Sage said sarcastically, then sighed. "I do have to admit I'm glad Mrs. Criter wasn't lying to me about the amount of care he would need. He pretty much takes care of himself. I caught him walking back from the bathroom this morning, so at least we know his legs work."

Noah raised an eyebrow. "So he's just being lazy?"

"I think apathetic is a better word." Sage removed the last of the chicken from the skillet. "Okay, lunch is ready. Let's see if the old man likes fried chicken." She placed a sturdy paper plate on the breakfast tray. "I'll wheel him outside. Could you follow me with the tray?"

Noah nodded as Sage knocked twice on Lucas's door. "Time for lunch," she said opening the door.

Lucas sat in the same spot she had placed him in that morning staring at the bird feeders.

"I've got a special treat for you today," said Sage. "Fried Chicken, homemade noodles and Jell-O salad. You must be hungry since we skipped breakfast."

Sage released the brake, and Lucas grabbed onto the wheels.

"Oh no, mister," said Sage. "It's a beautiful day, and you're eating outside. It's a good chance for you to soak up some rays, and if you decide you don't care for lunch, the dog can eat it when you throw it across the yard. We named her Lexi, by the way."

Lucas grunted, but let go of the wheels. What was this woman trying to do to him? All he wanted to do was die. Silly woman should have left him to rot in some rundown adult ward. He didn't care what she did, he wasn't going to eat, and she couldn't make him.

Sage wheeled him into the yard facing the barn. At least she could've pointed me toward the lake, Lucas thought. I bet there's some pretty good sized trout in that lake. He pushed the thought away. He was here to die, not fish.

His stomach growled as Sage placed a tray filled with fried chicken, homemade noodles, mashed potatoes, and Jell-O salad in front of him. His mouth watered. How did she know this was his favorite meal?

"I'll leave you to try and eat on your own," said Sage. "I'll check on you in a few minutes to see if you need any help." She handed him a plastic fork and spoon.

Lucas heard the back door close, but he wasn't alone. In the barn doorway, sat a dog, licking her lips. Lucas eyed his food, then the dog. The dog inched closer.

Oh, this is rich. Cooper laughed, standing next to the dog. *She's got you eating outside where you belong. 'Bout time Sage came to her senses about you. Hey, devil dog, why don't you go steal that nasty man's fried chicken. He doesn't deserve it. Go ahead, girl.* Cooper coaxed.

Lucas watched Lexi look to her left, then inch a little closer. The dog seemed to be looking at something that he couldn't see. Lucas grabbed the tray and considered throwing it. The smell of chicken tickled his nose as noodle juice broke free of its mashed potato dam. No, he thought again, he was there to die.

Go ahead and get some chicken, coaxed Cooper to Lexi. *You can run faster than that wheelchair. But don't be surprised if he gets up running. He doesn't really need the chair. It's all an act. I've seen him walking. Go for it, girl. Get the chicken.* Cooper laughed as Lexi looked up at him again, eyes begging him to go get the chicken for her.

Lucas balanced the tray on the wheelchair arms. He couldn't explain it, but he thought he heard Cooper's laugh dance along the wind. As if on cue, a smell of roasted peanuts wafted through the air.

Lucas remembered watching Cooper eat bags and bags of the salty treat. Lucas grabbed a chicken leg. What if the dog was looking at the spirit of his son? Redhawks had been known to hang around long after their passing, especially if their spirits were restless. He'd heard stories that his Grandpa Joe still haunted the farm house he grew up in. Yes, Lucas thought, it had to be his son, and if his son was there, then he could mend the bridge he'd burned so long ago.

He took a big bite of the chicken and sighed. It reminded him of Cooper's mom. She had been an excellent cook too. His stomach rumbled in protest, and Lucas reminded himself to eat small bites. The last thing he wanted to do was puke up the best meal he'd had in ages.

"It's working," sang Sage watching Lucas out the window. "You're a freakin' genius."

"I have my moments," said Noah munching down a spoonful of potatoes. "Good Lord, Sage, you are a chef in your own right. Have you considered ditching this B&B idea and just opening a restaurant?"

Sage blushed. "Way too much work, takes all the fun out of cooking. I was a short order cook back in high school and hated every minute of it. It took a long time for me to pick up a spatula again. At least here I can cook what I want in the comfort of my dream kitchen." She looked around. "Well, it will be my dream kitchen as soon as the faucet gets fixed, the track lighting put in, and the …"

Noah held up his hand. "I get your point. There's a lot of work to be done and not a lot of time before the spring season." He scooped up the last bit of potatoes on his plate. "I expect leftovers for dinner you know." He winked at Sage.

"Absolutely," she said, taking his plate and hers to the sink.

Noah headed to the back door as a police truck rolled into the driveway.

"Sage," he called over his shoulder, "there's a police truck out here. Anything you need to tell me?"

Sage came to the door, drying her hands off with a towel. "It's only Richard, probably here to check you out. I'm actually surprised he didn't grill you on the first day. He really wanted to, but I talked him out of it."

"Should I have an attorney present?" asked Noah as Cooper appeared by his side.

I bet you have one on speed dial, said Cooper. *You can bet if you've done something wrong, Park will know. The man is like a walking lie detector. I should know, he's grilled me enough times.*

Sage laughed. "You'll be fine. Let me finish putting these leftovers away, and I'll be out. Go say 'hi'."

Noah reluctantly gave Sage a nod. He'd much rather deal with the leftovers than have to talk to the current "living" alpha male in Sage's life, especially a cop. Noah had nothing to hide as far as a criminal past, but glancing at Cooper, Noah knew he definitely had something to hide as far as Sage went. Taking the steps two at a time, he walked out to meet Richard.

Chapter 15

Noah extended his hand to the approaching officer. "You must be Richard. Sage has told me a lot about you. She'll be right out. I'm Noah Finnley."

Don't be fooled. He already knows your name and your whole life story. If you've jaywalked in the past, he knows it. Cooper rubbed his hands together. *This is going to be good.*

Richard raised an eyebrow and took Noah's hand in a firm grip. "Sage calls me Richard. You can call me Deputy Park."

Cooper let out a hardy laugh.

"Understood," said Noah, tightening his grip on the handshake. "I know you and Sage go way back."

Richard let go. "You could say that." He looked at the house. "I see you got the new roof on. That the blizzard didn't get the best of you."

I'm amazed you got it up when you can't even stay on a ladder. Cooper leaned into Richard. *Damn fool almost killed himself.*

"No, sir, finished up this morning," said Noah, wondering why he had added the 'sir' part. Must have been the badge. "The blizzard and trip to Sap Springs kept me off the roof a couple of days, but as soon as things got settled, I finished the job. I always finish what I've started."

"What trip?" Richard rubbed his jaw, before looking at Lucas. "And who's that?"

"Lucas Redhawk," Noah answered. "Cooper's father and the reason for the trip."

Cooper's lip curled. *Now, he's the one you need to arrest. Just take him away and dump him alongside the freeway. No one will miss him.*

Richard pulled a toothpick out of his hat and stuck it in his mouth. "Cooper's father is dead."

"Apparently not," said Noah. "It's not really my story to tell. If you'll excuse me, I need to see if Lexi will let me into the barn to take some measurements."

Y'all named the devil dog, Lexi? Satan or Spawn or even Cujo are more fitting names, said Cooper.

"Lexi?" Richard chewed on the toothpick.

"The dog," answered Noah.

"The feral one?"

That's putting it mildly.

"I don't know if feral is the right word. She keeps her distance, but she's warming up to us." Noah extended his hand again. "Nice to meet ya."

Richard gave it a quick shake before turning toward the back door Sage had just exited.

"I see you met Noah?" she said giving Richard a hug.

He nodded. "I have."

"Did you eat?" asked Sage, "I just put up our lunch, but I'd be more than happy to fix you a plate."

"I ate in town, but thanks, Sage," said Richard, looking around the property.

Noah started toward the barn.

"No need to run off, Noah" said Sage. "You can help me show Richard all the improvements you've made. Did you see the roof?"

Ahhhh... let him go. You're gonna give him the wrong impression, like he's needed. And he's not.

Richard nodded. "I did."

"I think Deputy Park would prefer to catch up with you without me tagging along," said Noah.

"Deputy Park?" Sage rolled her eyes. "Call him Richard like everyone else. The only ones that call him Deputy Park are criminals."

Cooper clapped his hands, letting out another loud laugh. *He's got you pegged, huh, Finnley?*

Noah raised an eyebrow.

"Not only did I notice the roof," Richard said, changing the subject, "but I noticed an old man in a wheelchair. Mr. Finnley tells me he's Cooper's father."

Sage nodded. "Yes, I was pretty surprised myself to find out Coop's father is still alive. He was in a nursing home up in Sap Springs, so I went and got him."

"Why didn't you call me first? I could've done a background check before you made the trip. It's quite a coincidence that Cooper's father just happens to show up not long after Mr. Finnley here," said Richard.

That's right, Richard. Kick them both out, they deserve it.

Noah felt his face flush. "I'm not sure what you're getting at, Deputy Park."

"Well, let me be blunt." Richard turned to Sage. "How do you know these two aren't working together? Now you're out here all alone with two men. There's no telling what they could do to you."

Cooper shrugged. *That's what I've been saying all along.*

"Richard, calm down," said Sage, narrowing her eyes at Richard.

Oh, crap, said Cooper looking at Sage. *I know that look. He's about to get it. Guess you and the wheelchair man are sticking around. I knew Richard wouldn't be able to handle Sage. She always did have him wrapped around her little finger. Of course, who am I to talk? I would've walked to the moon had she asked.*

"Noah knew nothing of Lucas. Coop paid for Lucas to stay in Sap Springs thinking we would never see him again. Had the lady at the home not tracked down the insurance claim I filed and gotten my number from *you*, I still wouldn't know Lucas was alive. But he is, and he's family." She looked at Noah. "And for the record, Richard, Noah has been very helpful. He did that entire roof by himself and in the middle of winter. He has been nothing but a gentleman. Trust me, I've met his sister, one false move, and she'll be all over him like a dog on a rabbit."

"Speaking of dogs," Richard started.

"Lexi is fine. She's warming up to us. This was her house first. We all have to adjust." Sage crossed her arms. "Richard, you've known me a long time. I've never been helpless, and I'm not starting now. I trust Noah, and I know I'm doing right by Coop by letting his father stay here. You've always been a good friend to me, but around here I'm boss. What I say goes. And I say Noah, Lucas, and the dog are staying. If you don't like it, you can leave."

Anyone have a white flag? I'd say Richard's a goner.

Richard held up his hands, palms facing her. "Okay, Sage. I'm just looking out for you. Truce?"

Sage nodded. "Of course, now let me show you around."

Noah watched Sage point to the roof again as she walked off with Richard. He was thankful she had stood up for him, but he couldn't shake the feeling that Richard was trouble.

"What do you really know about him?" Noah asked Cooper.

I've known that man since high school. I know for a fact he'd never put Sage in danger, which is a lot more than I can say about you. By the way, Sage won't have any problems with the devil dog. She and I have come to an understanding.

Noah nodded and made his way to Lucas who was still eating his brunch. "That woman can fry a mean chicken."

Lucas nodded quickly before shoving some Jell-O in his mouth. Lexi peeked her head out the barn door again, brown eyes begging Lucas to drop something.

While Richard is inside with Sage, let me show you what I meant, said Cooper.

Cooper appeared next to Lexi and gestured toward the dog as if saying to Noah, "See I told you you had nothing to worry about."

Lexi looked at Cooper with a slight snarl. Lucas tilted his head toward the spot where Cooper stood.

"So you've made friends with the dog?" Noah asked Cooper, but faced Lucas, just in case Lucas couldn't actually see Cooper.

"Friends" is a pretty strong word, but she tolerates me now, answered Cooper. *Can he see me? He's staring at me now, and he did it earlier, too.*

Noah nodded and bent to talk to Lucas. "I want to help you get better. I think I can help you mend some bridges from your past . . . with your son."

Noah waited for Lucas's reaction. When he got none, he continued. "It has to be our secret though. You can't let Sage know. There's too much baggage there."

Baggage? Cooper cried. *You don't think there's baggage between me and my old man? There's a whole freakin' luggage set. I don't want to 'reconnect' with that bastard. I want you to talk to Sage for me. Why would you tell him and not Sage?*

Noah ignored him and continued to talk to Lucas. "She misses him too much to move on. I'm afraid it will only hurt her. I will do this for you because I believe it will only help, not hurt. That you won't be too attached to his spirit to let him move on. Maybe you can help me convince him to go to the light.

"In return, I need you to be nicer to Sage. No throwing food, trays, or anything else. You don't have to like her, but you do have to appreciate what she's doing for you, and I'll do what I can to help you. Is that something you can live with?"

Lucas looked up at Noah and gave a long, slow nod.

"Okay," said Noah, "let's start with the basics. Can you see him?"

Lucas shook his head no and pointed to Noah.

"Yeah, I can see him. Though I wish I couldn't." Noah rubbed his jaw. "Can you hear him?"

Lucas again shook his head and pointed at Noah.

"Yes, I can hear him too," Noah admitted. "You're staring at him now, even though you say you can't see him. How do you know he's there?"

Lucas pointed to his heart.

Oh, that's classic. Cooper laughed. *He can feel me in his heart. Where the hell was all this heartfelt crap when my mom was still alive? Ask him that.*

"You know he's really angry with you?" asked Noah. "This may take a while."

Lucas finally dropped his eyes from where Cooper stood. Noah grabbed the tray and headed back to the house leaving Lucas alone with his thoughts.

"He has every right to be," Lucas whispered.

Chapter 16

"So, what's on your agenda today?" Sage asked Noah as she packed up her photography equipment.

"Well, the roof is fixed, the porch swing replaced, and all the porch rails complete. The countertops and kitchen cabinets are in, so we can either start renovating the kitchen, which will take a while, or we can start on the guest rooms or start replacing fixtures and faucets, or replace the upstairs floors. There's no shortage of options."

I don't hear you adding "fixing up the barn so you can move out" to that list, Cooper sneered.

"Kitchen," said Sage, "then faucets. I can start painting the guest rooms while you're working on that. I'd like to paint before you replace the floors and fixtures." She grabbed her bag. "I'll only be gone for an hour or so. I just want to take some pictures for Winter Song and get them uploaded to the printers today so I can frame them." She headed toward the door.

"Where are your bells?" asked Noah.

Bells? Cooper laughed. *A. all the bears are hibernating and B. no native of this country would be caught dead in bells.*

Sage rolled her eyes. "You can't be serious."

"I am." Noah narrowed his eyes. "We've been in a drought, and it's a mild winter. They are coming out of their dens early for food since they didn't have a lot of fat going into their sleep. I heard some men talking about it at the hardware store. The Game and Fish had to relocate one about a week ago because it was digging through trash at one of the ski lodges."

Sage held up her hand. "I've lived here my entire life. I'm well aware of the grizzly danger. If I wear bells on my shoes then that scares away everything. I'll be careful, I promise. You better watch out, Noah Finnley, or I'll start to think you like me."

Where the hell did that come from? asked Cooper.

Sage gave herself a mental brain slap and headed out the door before Noah could respond. What was she doing? Flirting? How could she flirt with another man? She was in love with Cooper.

She slung on her backpack and placed the camera around her neck as she started down the lake trail.

Making her way through the trail, she stopped to take pictures of Bear Lake and a small fox hidden in the brush. Nothing made her happier than hiking in the forest. The birds called out, and she snapped a quick picture of a bald eagle before it soared over the lake.

"Not sure that one will come out," she said to herself. "I'll have to tell Noah the eagles are here. He might want to see them."

Ugh, I can't believe you were flirting with that guy back there, Cooper said, gliding along the path beside her.

No wonder he won't tell you he can see me. You're letting him believe he has a chance.

Sage stopped and looked at her feet. "I'm sorry, Coop."

Wait, Cooper stepped in front of her. *Can you see me? Maybe this thing is catching? First Noah, then the dog and my dad, and now you...*

Sage walked through him.

Or maybe not. Cooper sighed.

"It's just I don't know what to feel. My brain tells me you're gone forever. I mean I know you're never coming back."

Oh, baby, but I am. I'm right here.

"I just can't shake the feeling that every harmless flirt is cheating on you. And the funny thing is, I don't want anyone else but you, Coop." She wiped her eyes. "Of course, I don't want to be alone either. I swear I'll never forgive you for getting on that ship. I told you not to go. Why couldn't you just listen to me?"

Sage inhaled deeply. "Get it together, Sage. You did nothing wrong. You are a single lady who made a comment to a single man. It doesn't mean you're gonna have his babies. So what if you're flirting a little bit? You're allowed to find a handsome man attractive."

I think I'm gonna puke.

"Just don't let it go too far," she continued. "He is your employee. Now it's time to get these pictures done and head back to Winter Song. There's still so much work to be done."

A rustle in the huckleberry bushes grabbed her attention. Whatever it was, it was big.

Time to go, Sage, Cooper said. He grabbed for her hand, but once again his hand passed right through hers.

Sage took a step toward the rustling and raised her camera.

Bad idea, baby. Let's go, Cooper pleaded.

Sage took another step as a grizzly stood up on its hind legs, swallowing Sage in her shadow. A dead elk lay behind the angry bear.

"Whoa, bear," Sage cooed, releasing the camera and holding up her hands. "I'm leaving now. You can have that elk all to yourself. I don't want it. It's all yours." She slowly backed from the bear, head down keeping the beast in her peripheral vision.

Cooper glanced from Sage to the bear. He could try to stop the bear, but if he had the same effect on the bear he had on the dog, it would just piss her off more. He appeared behind the bear and started screaming. *Over here, bear. I'm gonna eat your elk.*

Unfazed by Cooper, the animal continued to stalk Sage. Cooper stood feeling helpless. He'd wait, if the bear attacked Sage, he'd get Noah. Maybe the sow would let her go.

The bear charged toward Sage, stopping after a few feet, pawing violently at the ground, while letting out an angry snort. Sage stood her ground.

"Just let me go bear." She took another couple of steps backward.

The bear charged again. Sage knew the bear wasn't bluffing this time. She waited for the right moment to hit the ground and play dead, hoping the dead part wouldn't become a reality. When the bear was a foot away, Sage dropped to the ground, curled up into a fetal position and covered her ears and head with her arms. She waited for the bear's paws to rip into her sides. She could hear snarls and heavy breathing, but there was something else. Was that barking? And a yelp, she definitely heard a yelp. Could it be Lexi?

Sage wanted to open her eyes to see if it was indeed Lexi, but didn't dare. She knew grizzlies would lurk in the shadows to see if their prey was bluffing and then attack again. The snarls had stopped, and she no longer smelled the musky scent of the creature, but she was still afraid to move. She felt hot breath on her face and then the cold wet lick of a tongue briefly touched her hand. She glanced over her forearm. There stood Lexi, panting, a cut above one eye, but okay.

Sage sat up and slowly reached up to pet the dog. Lexi stepped into her hand and nuzzled her face, licking Sage's cheek.

Cooper paced around them. *You'd never believe it. The dog just came out of nowhere and attacked the bear. The sow just took off, leaving the elk behind. I wanted to stop the bear myself, but she'd just run right through me, and I didn't want to tick her off any more than she already was. I can't believe devil dog saved your life.*

"Thank you, Lexi," Sage said rubbing the dog behind the ears. "I owe you one."

Lexi took off back along the trail toward Winter Song and looked at Sage to follow.

"I believe you're right," said Sage. "We've had enough hiking for one day."

Noah flew out of the house after seeing a bloody Lexi come out of the trail followed closely by a limping Sage.

"What happened?" he asked, trying to judge if Lexi would let him look at the eye without biting. "Are you okay, Sage?"

She's fine. If you care so much about her, talk to her for me, huffed Cooper.

"I'm fine. I twisted my ankle a bit when I hit the ground. You were right, I should've worn bells," said Sage.

Noah rubbed his jaw. "You ran into a grizzly?"

Sage nodded. "Would've been bear meat if it hadn't been for Lexi."

She rubbed the dog's head.

Noah looked at Cooper to confirm. *Yes, the devil dog saved the day.*

Noah bent down and held out his hand for Lexi to sniff as Lucas rolled up behind them.

"Lucas, it's so good to see you moving around," said Sage. "Come meet the hero of the day. Lexi here saved me from a bear, and she's decided to be friends with us."

Lucas stared at Lexi. She titled her head as she studied him.

"Good dog," Lucas said and then wheeled away, Lexi trailing behind him.

"Lucas," yelled Sage, "what did you say? Come back here. We need to talk about this."

Ignoring her, Lucas continued to wheel himself toward the lake.

Noah looked at Sage. "Well I'll be, the old bugger can talk."

Great, as if just having him around wasn't enough fun, Cooper said with a sneer.

Sage shrugged. "Doesn't surprise me one bit."

"It doesn't?" Noah raised an eyebrow.

"Cooper could go days without talking to me if he was mad enough. He had to get it from somewhere," said Sage, heading toward the house.

And that's about the only thing we have in common, Cooper chimed in.

"I'm gonna put my things away and get started on painting the upstairs," said Sage, going up the back stairs and into the house.

"Are you sure you're okay?" asked Noah. "Maybe you should rest? Or maybe we should call Deputy Park?"

"I'm fine," said Sage. "And there's no need to call Richard. I'll catch up with you later on the kitchen progress."

As soon as Sage was out of earshot, Noah looked at Cooper. "What exactly were you doing during this bear attack?"

Cooper held up his hands. *I didn't do anything, and it just about killed me.*

"Ha, ha," said Noah, dryly.

No, seriously. I wanted to stand in front of the bear, scare it off, do something, but then I thought of how the devil dog reacted to me. I didn't know if the sow would react the same way. So I just stood to the side, helpless. Cooper kicked at the ground, a small rock bounced away.

"I was laughing at the 'just about killed me part'." Noah furrowed his brow. "You know, because you're already dead."

Cooper scowled at Noah. *Very funny, pal.*

Noah turned to go into the house.

"Is it true?" asked Noah, over his shoulder. "What she said about you not talking to her for days when you were mad."

Cooper dropped his head. *Yeah, but I'd take all those pissed off moments back in a heartbeat if I could just tell her I love her one more time.* He looked at Noah. *You know you could do that for me. She has to know how much she meant to me. How much I regret those times I took for granted.*

"Will you go into the light?" asked Noah.

I made her a promise that I'd never leave her again. I'm not breaking one more promise to her.

"Then the only messages I'll be relaying are to your father." Noah rubbed his neck. "You got anything you want to say to him?"

Hell, no, said Cooper.

"Well, then," said Noah, "I guess this conversation is over."

Cooper watched Noah walk into the house before he turned toward the lake. There sat Lucas, bending over Lexi, gently cleaning her cut with a handkerchief. The cut clean, Lucas rolled himself down the trail a bit, leaving Lexi sitting by the lake. Cooper went to her.

I owe you a belly rub, devil dog, he said as he sat next to her. *I'm not sure what would've happened had you not come when you did. Thanks, girl.*

Lexi laid next to him, and they both stared out at the lake until Cooper broke the silence. *I've spent almost a year following Sage around, my sole purpose to make sure she never felt alone or afraid. I want to protect her, but it turns out I'm pretty useless at it.* He sighed. *Turns out I was pretty useless at a lot of things. She was right, you know?*

Lexi cocked her head.

I would get so mad at her over the smallest things, like if she had to pull a double at work or if she wanted to vacuum the living room while the Broncos were playing. We're talking super trivial things here, devil dog. And I would pout and not talk to her for days. It seems so ridiculous now. And now that I finally know how foolish I was, I can't tell her how sorry I am. She is the best thing that ever happened to me. I would give anything to be able to tell her that one last time. I would give anything for her to hear me say, "I love you" one last time.

Chapter 17

Noah spent the next few days trying to figure out how to talk to Sage. She was acting like the bear incident never happened. It wasn't like he'd never encountered a bear on a hike before, but he was worried about animals of another form--the human one.

Sage was going to be letting strangers sleep in her house with nothing but a dead bolt and a crippled old man standing between her and some lunatic. Sure, the majority of the people booking rooms at a bed and breakfast weren't going to be the menacing type, but he was sure there would be someone thinking it was an opportunity. Once he moved into the barn, she would be very vulnerable. Maybe they should get some walkie-talkies or some kind of radio system from the house to the barn.

Noah met Sage coming out of the barn.

"It's looking good in there," she said. "The floors are really nice. Wish I would've picked that for the upstairs. Can't believe how much you've gotten done while working on the main house as well."

"Thanks."

"I really am impressed," Sage continued. "I mean the man at the hardware store said you were good, but this is just outstanding. We're going to be finished way ahead of schedule at this rate. I just know one day you're going to come to your senses and find a real job."

"This is a real job," said Noah, rubbing his jaw and looking around for Cooper. He didn't seem to be anywhere around, which was odd since he usually followed Sage around like a puppy.

"Uh-oh," said Sage, frowning.

"What?"

"Every time you rub your jaw or neck it means you're worried about something," she said.

"You've noticed that about me?" he raised an eyebrow.

"I notice a lot of things." She closed her eyes. "Out with it. What's wrong with Winter Song now?"

"Actually, it has very little to do with Winter Song," he said.

Sage opened her eyes. "Really? I just knew you were going to say we needed to replace the electrical too."

"Look, Sage." Noah started pacing. "We've been working together for a few months, and I think we've got a good thing going here…"

"Oh, crap. You've already found a real job. I knew this was all too good to be true. You're quitting, aren't you?" She leaned against the door frame to steady herself.

"No, I'm not quitting," said Noah, "I'm not going anywhere. I don't think you're going to like what I have to say, but keep in mind it's coming from a place of concern."

"Go on then," said Sage, folding her arms. "You know you can talk openly with me."

"Once I move out here, you'll be alone in the house with the guests," Noah explained.

"I don't know how 'alone' I'll be, but I get your point."

"Well," continued Noah, "I'm just concerned that someone will cause trouble, and you won't be able to defend yourself."

Sage burst out with a strong belly laugh. "That's your concern? Really, it's not a problem."

"Just like the bear wasn't a problem?" Noah's face turned red. "Look, I understand the deal was for me to stay out here. You need the room for boarders. I get that. I just think we need to find a way for you to protect yourself."

"So you think I'm a damsel in distress?" She smirked.

"That's not what I said."

"I'm just a little girl," Sage started speaking with an exaggerated southern accent, as she walked toward him. "How will I ever get through this big bad world without a big, strong man to save me?"

"Sage, I'm just concerned. I care about your safety."

"Let's get one thing straight right here, right now, Noah Finnley. I don't need anyone to take care of me."

"And just what are you going to do if a guy attacks you looking for money? Hit him with your hairbrush?" Noah mocked.

"No. This."

Sage grabbed Noah by the arm, twisted him around until he fell to his knees. His shoulder ached as she pulled back.

"Good Lord, woman," he yelled.

She let go of his arm. "You think I worked as night manager at that flea bag hotel and didn't get myself some self-defense classes? I'm no black belt, but I can take care of myself. Besides I'll be screaming loud enough to wake the dead, and then you can come running to my rescue."

Noah stood and brushed off his knees. "I thought you didn't need to be rescued. Wasn't that the point of your little Kung Fu move?"

"Well," said Sage, batting her eyelids, "I want you to feel needed. Isn't that what every man wants . . ." She leaned in close. ". . . to save a woman?"

He leaned into her. "Do you need saving?"

She let out a slow breath but didn't move. Her eyes glanced at his lips making his heart beat faster. She tilted her head up and moistened her lips. His instinct took over before his brain could object, and he swallowed her in a hard kiss. He placed his hands lightly on her hips, giving her the option to back away. To his surprise, she threw her arms around his neck and gave into the kiss fully.

He wrapped his arms around her waist and took her in completely. He fought the urge to pick her up and carry her straight to the master bedroom. She broke away, catching her breath and looking him squarely in the eyes. He stared back, so desperately wanting to tell her that he was here for the long haul. That this was serious to him. He tried to read her face. Was she serious about him?

Neither spoke. Suddenly the light over the barn glowed hot with energy, bursting the bulb and light cover, causing them both to jump.

"Maybe I need to replace the electric after all," Noah said softly and then laughed.

But Sage didn't laugh back, instead she stepped away. "Oh, my God, what have I done?" Her hand covered her mouth as she continued to back up toward the house. "We shouldn't have done that. I'm sorry, but that can't happen again." She turned and ran toward the house.

Noah watched her go, his heart racing. He started after her as a small rock pelted him in the back. He turned expecting to see Lucas, but found Cooper instead. Noah's face flushed with color. "Damn it, Cooper, that is exactly why you need to go into the light! She will never move on with you lurking in the shadows."

And let you steal my woman? Cooper threw another rock.

Noah stood his ground, the rock bouncing off his chest. "You're dead! You've been dead for almost a year. For the love of God, let Sage move on."

You mean move on with you? Cooper tried to pick up a larger rock, but his hand washed right through it. His energy was spent.

Noah sighed and lowered his voice. "Would that be so bad? I would never do anything to hurt Sage. I want nothing more than for her to be happy."

She was happy with me. Cooper snarled.

"Was, Cooper. You can't make her happy any more. You're only making it worse. Can't you see that?" Noah put his hands together and concentrated on the barn door, where the light had once again appeared. "Please, Cooper, go into the light. Do it for Sage."

You mean do it for you. Cooper looked at the light in disgust and then looked up. *I will go into light when Sage goes with me. Do you hear that, you son of a bitch?* he yelled to the sky. The light disappeared.

Noah shook his head. "You're only going to make her miserable."

You're the one I'm going to make miserable. Cooper snapped. *You better back off or you'll be sorry. You caught me off guard with that punch at Pleasant Valley, you won't be that lucky again.*

Noah shrugged. "I'll take my chances."

He turned toward the house. Right now he had a relationship to fix with Sage. The last thing he was worried about was a pebble-throwing ghost.

Chapter 18

Sage cursed herself as she pried open the paint can. How could she let herself kiss Noah? It was irresponsible. He was her employee, her handyman, and a darn good one at that. He could definitely sue her for sexual harassment if he wanted too. Just how many labor laws had she broken with one kiss?

And then there was Cooper. How could she kiss another man? Cooper had been the only man to touch her lips that way. She moistened her lips, still tingling from the kiss. Her heart thudded loudly at the thought of her betrayal.

But was the kiss really a betrayal? thought Sage. Cooper was dead. She would never get to kiss those lips again. Just because he was her soul mate, the only man she had ever dated or loved, didn't mean she couldn't have feelings for another man. It didn't mean she had to become a nun. She was a woman with feelings and needs.

Cooper's face flashed through her mind, "No," she said softly, there was only one love for her. This thing with Noah couldn't happen. It was too complicated.

She heard Noah taking the stairs two at a time, and she stirred the paint. Best to act as if nothing happened, she thought. We just need to go back to the way things were. No harm, no foul, and everyone can go on their merry little ways to get Winter Song up and running.

"We need to talk about what just happened," Noah said, leaning on the door frame.

Sage shook her head. "No, we don't. We don't have to mention it ever again as far as I'm concerned."

"Sage, please," he begged, "we need to clear the air."

"Clear the air, huh?" She said, grabbing a paintbrush. "It was a mistake. I don't want to jeopardize our partnership here with romance. I just got caught up in the moment. It's nothing personal. We are business partners, and we need to keep it that way, nothing else."

"But it is personal," Noah said, moving towards her and placing his hand on her shoulder. "What I felt out there--what we felt--was more than a business relationship. I know you felt it too."

Sage shrugged him off and dipped the paintbrush into a calming soft turquoise color, wishing it would calm her nerves. "I'll be the first to admit I was caught up. I mean, who wouldn't be?" She pointed the paintbrush at him, gesturing to Noah's physique. "You're hot and nice and good looking and helpful, everything a girl looks for in a man." She shook her head, not sure she was proving her point. "I'm just not in a place where I am free to be in a relationship."

"Because of Cooper?"

Sage nodded. "I still love him. I will never stop. I'm not sure there's room for someone else, and that's not fair to you."

"I understand." Noah crossed his arms. "But, I don't believe you should never find anyone else because of your love for Cooper. I do understand you need more time. And I'll wait. I'll wait for you. Until then, I'm not going anywhere."

Sage went back to her painting. "I'm not going down that road with you, Noah, so there's no reason to wait. If it's too hard staying on here at Winter Song and helping out, I won't hold you to it."

"You're not getting out of this partnership that easy." He smiled.

That smile made her want to melt into his arms. But she knew it was a horrible idea that would only lead to more heartache. She had seen enough heartache for a lifetime. No need to put herself through more.

"So are you just going to stand there and smile all day or fix something?" she asked concentrating on her brush strokes.

Noah ran his hands through his hair. "I'll be downstairs working on the kitchen so you can have some space."

With that, he turned and walked down the stairs. Sage shook her head, trying to rid her mind of the kiss.

I can't believe you kissed that guy, said Cooper. *After all we've been through? The years we've put in together? You'd just throw it all away on a stupid carpenter. Why, Sage, why?*

Sage sighed and sat back on her knees. "Stop it," she said to herself. "You are not going to cry. There is no reason to cry."

But her tears didn't listen. Instead they started cascading down her cheeks. "Don't do this to yourself," she whispered. "Coop's dead. You did nothing wrong."

You kissed another man! Cooper yelled. *We've been together since middle school. Never once, did I kiss another girl. I was faithful to you every day of my life. Is it too much to ask you to do the same?*

Sage sat the paintbrush on the rim of the paint can and positioned herself cross-legged, leaning her head in her hands, still whispering, "I did nothing wrong. I can't bring Coop back. We can't be together now. We can't build this dream together, so why shouldn't I build it with someone else?"

Because this is our dream, baby. We've been planning this since high school. Why would you want to share it with anyone else? He brushed her hair off her shoulder. *How could you do this to me?*

Sage looked up and glanced around the room. No one was there. She dried her eyes and picked the paintbrush back up.

"Get yourself together, Sage," she said. "There's work to be done or there won't be a dream to share with anyone. Just stay focused on the work. Pretend it didn't happen."

I wish I could, said Cooper.

Noah heard Sage's soft sobs and fought the urge to run to her. He wanted to hold her and tell her everything would be all right. He wanted to explain that he wasn't trying to replace Cooper, but to convince her there was room for him as well. He wanted to kiss every tear off her cheeks. But he knew he couldn't. Knew the timing wasn't right.

If only Cooper hadn't seen the kiss and caused the light bulb and fixture to shatter. That ghost was getting more powerful every day, and Noah knew it was only a matter of time before Cooper did something to prove to Sage he was still hanging around. The longer Cooper stayed out of the light, the more energy he'd be able to harness. And if he got angry enough, he could become a full-fledged poltergeist. Noah had seen that kind of thing happen before. If that happened there would be no light for Cooper then.

Noah shook the thought away, a poltergeist was the last thing he needed to deal with. He had to find a way to get Cooper to walk into the light. Noah toyed with the notion of relaying Cooper's messages and shook that thought away too. If he started talking for him, Cooper would never leave, and he would become a human answering machine.

No, he had to get Cooper into the light. Noah looked out toward the lake, spotting Lucas staring at the blue waters. If he could mend that bridge, then just maybe he could get Cooper to move on.

But how? Cooper was adamant that he didn't want to have anything to do with his father. Noah stepped outside and made his way to Lucas.

"Any suggestions on how to get Cooper to listen?" Noah asked.

Lucas chuckled. "His mother used to say he was so stubborn that if he didn't want to move, even a tornado couldn't make him."

Noah scratched his head. "We really need him to go into the light soon."

"You are right. Moving on is important for everyone, but we must all have closure first," said Lucas.

"Does that mean you think I should talk to Sage for Cooper?" Noah didn't know if he really wanted to hear Lucas's answer.

"No . . . but . . .," said Lucas, ". . . helping Cooper move on will help Sage get closure. Still it never hurts to hear, 'I love you' one last time."

Noah took in Lucas's words. He had a lot to think about, and he could think while working. Besides keeping his hands busy would keep him from throwing the stubborn fool into the light. Grabbing his hammer, he shook his head.

Lord help him, he would not grab Cooper by the neck, as he had at the nursing home, and throw him into the light. It had to be Cooper's choice to go. Throwing him into the light wasn't an option as far as Noah was concerned. Cooper was a pain in the butt, but he belonged to Sage, and Noah respected Sage too much not to give Cooper the option of going into the light.

Chapter 19

Noah checked his watch again. It wasn't like Becca to be late. Sage laid a soft hand on his arm, sending tingles through his chest. It was the first time she had touched him since the kiss.

"They'll be here," she said. "Remember, your sister is traveling with two kids. It'll take her longer than it did us to get there, especially since they're not eating peanut butter and cayenne jelly sandwiches."

Noah laughed. "You're right. I guess I'm just a little nervous about them coming out."

"Why?" asked Sage. "I thought you'd be thrilled to have your sister and nieces here for a couple of days."

Noah wanted desperately to tell Sage exactly what worried him, that he was afraid Cooper would convince Kelly and Katie to relay messages to Sage. He was afraid Becca would slip up and out him as being a seer, not just a seer, but one who could see Cooper. Sage was already spooked after their kiss. One mention of her dead boyfriend still being around, and Noah would be toast.

"Well, these girls have no idea how to act around nature. What if they run into a bear?" Noah lied.

Sage tried to swallow a smile, but her dimple gave her away.

"Don't laugh," he said, "you were almost attacked."

"I know, but we're not going to let the girls go wandering around by themselves. They'll be safe here at Winter Song," Sage countered.

"If they ever get here." Noah looked at his watch again.

This time Sage didn't try to hide her smile. "Here they are now."

Becca's van pulled over the hill and into the drive. Noah could see Kelly sitting in the front seat waving wildly, while her sister Katie leaned forward from the backseat to get a better view.

The girls jumped out of the car before their mom had even put it in park. "Uncle Noah," they cried, "this place is amazing."

"Can we go swimming?" asked Kelly.

"I can't wait to go hiking," said Katie.

"Settle down, girls," said Becca, sliding out from behind the driver's seat. "We've got all weekend to explore." She smiled at Sage. "So good to see you again. Are you sure you're ready for this?"

"Of course," said Sage, "it'll be a nice trial run before the guests get here, and I could sure use the help painting."

"We get to paint!" squealed the girls.

"Let's just hope they keep that enthusiasm," said Noah.

Lucas wheeled up beside Sage.

"Becca, Kellie, Katie, this is Lucas," Sage introduced. "He lives here as well."

Becca shook his hand. "Cooper's father, right?"

"Did you learn that from Google as well?" asked Sage with a raised eyebrow.

Becca smiled. "That I learned from Noah."

"It is nice to meet you," said Lucas. "Please excuse me, my tired old bones need to lay down."

Sage checked her watch. "I'll help you in, Lucas. The pies are almost done. I better check on them."

"We'll be inside in a minute," said Noah. "I'll help Becca with the bags."

Noah watched Sage roll Lucas into the house before he spoke again. "So, you girls know the rules, right?"

The tweens rolled their eyes.

"No roaming off into the woods," said Kellie.

"No swimming without supervision," said Katie.

"Be nice to Sage," said Kellie.

"Help out and use our manners," said Katie.

The girls paused.

"And?" their mother prompted.

The girls glanced at each other and then repeated in unison. "Under no circumstances are we to talk to any ghosts or let Sage know we can see any ghosts."

"And what happens if you break that last rule?" asked Becca.

"Uncle Noah will get fired," said Kellie.

"And we will be grounded for all eternity," said Katie.

"You've got that right," said Becca.

Noah ran his hands through his hair. "All right then, let's get these bags, and I'll show you around."

Hey, hey, the gangs all here, said Cooper, as he appeared behind the van as the family gathered to collect their luggage.

Becca closed the distance between them. "Look, you know we can see you. There's nothing we can do about that. But Noah told me of your threat to haunt my girls if he didn't relay messages to Sage. Let's get one thing straight, buddy, no one threatens my girls, living or dead." She stuck her finger in his face. "You stay away from them, or I will find a way to get Sage to put Rowan on her door. I'll make her the prettiest damn wreath you'll ever see. Do we understand each other?"

"Oh, I've seen that look before," said Kellie.

"He better do as she says," said Katie.

Becca swirled around. "Girls, the rules!"

"What?" said Kellie, "We weren't talking to him."

"Don't talk about him either," said Becca.

Cooper held up his hands. *I get it, and I'm sorry. It was wrong of me to threaten your girls. I am desperate to talk to Sage. I need her to know I haven't left her. That I've kept my promise to come back to her.*

"Talk is cheap where I come from, Cooper. As much as I appreciate your apology, I need your word that you'll leave them alone. I need you to make the same kind of promise to me about my daughters as you did regarding staying with Sage."

If I do, will you talk to her for me? asked Cooper.

"I will definitely think about it." Becca turned to her brother and shrugged. "Well at least he apologized."

"But," said Noah to Cooper, "will you go into the light and let Sage move on if she talks to her for you?"

Not on your life, pal.

"And now you see our problem," said Noah. "We better get these bags inside before Sage starts to wonder what we're doing out here."

"Maybe I should talk to Sage," said Becca. "She has a right to know what's happening."

Finally, said Cooper, *someone who understands and is willing to help.*

"Becca, I will lose my job," said Noah.

"Not if I tell her I can see him and relay the messages," explained Becca. "She doesn't have to know you can see him too, and maybe Cooper will leave you alone after he can say good-bye."

"I can't let you do that. Remember what happened to Mom? What if the same thing happens?" said Noah.

"What happened to Grandma?" asked Katie.

"We'll talk about it later," said Becca.

But you will talk to Sage? asked Cooper.

"We'll talk about all of it later. Now is not the time," said Becca. "Until I decide, will you respect what I've asked and leave my girls alone?"

Scouts honor. Cooper held up three fingers.

Cooper watched Noah and his family gather their bags and head inside Winter Song before he moseyed down to the lake. Lexi ran up and sat beside him.

This could be it, devil dog. I might finally be able to tell Sage I'm here. He rubbed his hands together. *I've been waiting for this day for such a long time. Who would've thought Finnley's sister would be so understanding? I thought I was going to have to make one of the girls slip up and out me.*

Lexi grumbled.

Hey, I didn't want to go there. I wasn't going to do anything hurtful to the girls. Just make them laugh or jump or something hard to explain. Sage has to know I'm still here.

The dog sighed and laid down.

I know I say it all the time, but it's the truth. We were meant to be together.

The dog tilted her head and let out a little whine.

Yes, I realize I'm being selfish. I'm dead, and she isn't, I get it. Is it too much for me to want her to pine away for me until the day she dies? Cooper paused and shook his head. *You're right. It is too much for me to ask. I do want her to be happy. I guess I'm just not ready to see her with another man. I don't know that I ever will be.*

Chapter 20

Becca and Noah hiked along the lake, the girls a few steps in front of them.

"Watch for bears," yelled Becca as the girls chased a dragonfly, trying to get a close-up picture.

"Are you really going to relay Cooper's messages?" asked Noah.

"Unless you give me a good reason not to," said Becca.

"How about Mom and my job?" Noah grabbed a leaf off a low branch and started picking at it.

"Don't do that," said Becca.

"Do what?" asked Noah.

"It's not about you," said Becca. "This is about Sage and Cooper. It is my understanding that they were together since middle school. How can you expect them not to have a connection after death? And this isn't Mom. I'm not going to be around twenty-four seven to relay messages. They'll have their closure, and then it's over."

"Becca, you heard him say he's not going into the light," answered Cooper. "He's gonna stick around."

"So what if he does? What's it to you? This is just a job, right?"

Noah locked his jaw, afraid of the answer that might come out.

"Noah, it is just a job, right?" Becca stopped her brother. "Look at me and tell me you haven't fallen for her."

"C'mon, Becca," said Noah, rubbing his neck. "Look at her. Just... she's... just look at her. And when I'm around her, I feel... well, I feel like everything is right."

"Ahh, for the love of Pete, you can be so stupid sometimes." Becca threw up her arms and started walking again. "Girls, not so far ahead."

Noah hurried to catch up with her. "It just kind of happened."

"What just kind of happened? Have you slept with her? With Cooper around? I can't even imagine, doing that with the spirit of the dead boyfriend watching." Becca shivered.

"No, we haven't slept together," said Noah. "But we kissed."

"Kissed, as in one kiss?"

Noah nodded.

"And does she want more?" asked Becca.

"She says she doesn't, but I think she's just confused."

"Sage doesn't strike me a woman who is confused," said Becca.

"She feels guilty for kissing me when she still loves Cooper. She can never be with him again. I'm not going to let her waste away pining after a man she can't have." Noah threw the leaf on the ground. "It isn't fair to her, and it isn't right for Cooper to keep that kind of hold over her. If she knows he's here, she'll never move on."

Becca crossed her arms. "I see your point. But, Noah, as long as you're lying to her, the two of you can never move forward. You're holding her back as much as Cooper is."

"How am I holding her back?" asked Noah.

"By not giving her a chance to say good-bye."

"She said good-bye at the funeral, Becca. Why would I want to drag her through that again?"

"Because this time Cooper can say good-bye back. It never really feels like good-bye when only one person says it. Knowing it's truly over, that he's truly on the other side will be her closure. And having that closure will give her heart the permission to move on with you."

Noah stopped to let his sister's words sink in.

"So are you going to tell her?" he hollered toward his sister.

Becca shrugged. "I'll let you know when I know."

Sage tossed the used sandpaper on top of the dresser and rubbed her shoulder. The dresser was going to look fantastic in one of the guest rooms, but first she had to get all the god-forsaken powder blue paint off so she could stain it a nice blonde.

"Need some help?"

Sage turned to see Becca. "I wouldn't mind a bit of a break, if you don't mind a bit of sanding."

Becca grabbed a fresh piece of sandpaper. "It comes with a price."

"Well, if it's money you're looking for, you're out of luck," laughed Sage.

Becca shook her head and began sanding. "A higher price than that I'm afraid."

"Okay," Sage said slowly.

"I was wondering if you'd talk to me about Cooper."

"Cooper?" Sage brushed the bangs out of her face. "I already know you Googled me, so you know what happened to him. I'm not sure what else you'd want to know."

"Well," said Becca, "I would like to know about your relationship with him."

"Why?" Sage bit her lip, knowing she sounded defensive. "I mean, it's personal."

"Because I know about the kiss with Noah," said Becca with a small smile, "and that makes it personal to me as well. I don't want to see my brother get hurt."

"First off, the kiss was a mistake. It's been a long time since Cooper passed, and I just got caught up in the moment. I'm not trying to take advantage of Noah. We work together, and I value his help and his friendship. It won't happen again. But I'm still not seeing what that has to do with Cooper."

"Okay," said Becca, "you know I'm just looking out for Noah."

"I get that," said Sage, "but we both know Cooper is dead."

Becca nodded. "I was in love with a ghost once."

"Huh?" Sage raised an eyebrow.

"The girls' father," explained Becca.

Sage's hand flew up to her mouth. "I'm so sorry, I didn't know. Noah made it sound like he was just a deadbeat dad."

"Oh, he is," said Becca. "The rat isn't dead."

"You've lost me," said Sage.

"I was in love with the person he used to be. When I first met their father, he was romantic and sweet. He had a full time job and bought us that house. He was a great father, spent every moment he could with the girls."

"What happened?" asked Sage.

"A girl by the name of Addy Pendergraph happened. They worked together. One thing lead to another, and soon they were sleeping together. Then one day he left for work and went home with her instead. After that, he started another family, and now he barely sees the girls."

"I'm so sorry, but I'm still not sure what that has to do with Cooper and me," said Sage.

"Well, for a long time, I lived in the past. I wouldn't date another man, and the one time I did manage a date, it ended in a kiss. I felt so guilty. I felt as if I had cheated on the rat. It was so silly. I mean, he left me, and here I was becoming a hermit because I wanted the man he used to be. But that man was dead." She looked up at Sage. "See where I'm going now?"

Sage nodded. "Cooper and I had been together for a long time. I'm not sure how to live without him. When I got the news..." Sage stopped. "What day is it?"

"Saturday, the 14th. Why?" answered Becca.

Tears flooded Sage's eyes. "Oh, my God, I can't believe I forgot."

She turned and ran into the barn, Becca close on her heels. "Forgot what?"

Sage turned into Becca and buried her head into her shoulder. "I forgot. Today's the anniversary of Cooper's death, and I forgot."

Becca rubbed Sage's back. "It's okay. You've been busy. It's easy to lose track of days."

Sage pulled away. "Not this day! How could I forget? What kind of person forgets the day her soulmate dies? I'm a monster."

Becca pulled her in. "You're no monster, Sage. You're human. It's okay to cry. Go ahead. You'll find no judgement here."

Sage's heart broke into a million pieces as she sobbed into Becca's shirt. It hurt, it hurt as if it had just happened. It hurt because he was gone, and it hurt even more that she had forgotten, but mostly it just hurt.

Chapter 21

Noah watched Becca and Sage embrace just outside the barn before Sage started up to the house. Her eyes were red and swollen, a sure sign that she had been crying. Waiting for Sage to walk into the house, he approached his sister.

"Is she okay?" he asked.

Becca nodded. "She will be. Did you know it's the anniversary date of Cooper's death?"

Noah sighed. "I had no idea. I should go talk to her."

He started to the house, but Becca pulled him back. "Don't. She needs to be alone right now. She needs to have her moment of grief, and we need to respect her enough to give her the privacy to do that properly. If you go up there, she's just going to put on a happy face and tell you everything is fine."

"So what do I do?" asked Noah, looking at the house. He longed to comfort Sage but knew his sister was right.

"We wait for her to decide the next move. She'll either go up there and have a good cry and be fine, or she'll want to wallow. If she wants to wallow, then I will bring her ice cream, and you will stay away. If she wants to pretend it's okay, we let her do that."

Noah turned to his sister. "And what about Cooper? Are you going to relay his messages?"

Becca shook her head. "I think you're right on this one. I don't know that she has it in her to let go if she knows he's here."

"That's not going to make Cooper happy," Noah said, thinking of the light fixture Cooper had broken during Sage and Noah's kiss.

"I'll explain it to him the best I can." Becca looked around the property. "Have you seen him today?"

Noah raised an eyebrow. "Come to think about it, I haven't."

The sun was warm, but Lucas shivered and pulled the blanket tighter around his body. He felt an imbalance in the universe, as if someone who was close to him was in imminent danger. Sage had just gone into the house from the barn, and Noah's family was all on the grounds, safe and sound. Everyone else he cared about was already on the other side.

His body shook in a wave of goose pimples. He felt as if he were floating on a boat. No, it was more violent than that. It was as if he was bobbing like an apple in a stormy sea. Grabbing his chest, he sucked in, unable to get a full breath. He wondered if this was what a heart attack felt like. If he hadn't been on land, he would've been sure he was drowning.

Finally taking a deep breath, he coughed, tasting salt water in his mouth. Noah ran up to him.

"Lucas, are you okay?"

Lucas managed a small nod, before gasping. "Have you seen Cooper? Must find Cooper."

Cooper felt as if he were sleeping in a hammock on a breezy day. The sensation was foreign to him. The entire time he'd been dead he'd never slept. But for some reason, while lying next to Sage the night before, watching her sleep as he had every night for almost a year, he felt tired.

Panic flooded his mind. This had to be something Noah was doing. Maybe he and his sister had concocted some kind of voodoo to make him go into the light. He fought to keep his eyes open, fought to hold onto Sage. The last thing he remembered was whispering 'I love you' to her as he drifted off.

A ringing started to form in the back of his mind. It was faint at first but grew louder. Soon it was ear-splitting. Cooper bolted up, quickly taking in his surroundings. He'd know this place anywhere. He was in his bunk on the *Fancy Nancy* cod boat.

"Maybe it was all a dream," Cooper whispered. "Maybe I haven't died, and this was all some weird *Wizard of Oz* stuff. I can get back to her." Cooper smiled. "I'm going home."

"Oh, my God. Oh, my God. Oh, my God," came a chant from the floor. It was Gavin Hart, Cooper's former bunkmate and fellow green horn.

Cooper hopped out of his bunk and grabbed the survival suits. "It's okay, kid. Just put on your suit. Probably just another drill. Trust me, no matter what, you're gonna be fine. But watch out for that nail on the floor. Don't catch your Gumby suit on it."

But Cooper knew it wasn't another drill. This time he could change things. This time both he and Gavin Hart would make it out alive.

Just as he had before, Cooper peeked his head into the galley. Smoke hazed through the cabin as Captain Mullis ran through the galley to get back to the wheelhouse. "Put on your suit, Davis, and then get up on deck and get the life raft ready. We're gonna need it."

"Captain, you should put on your suit," said Cooper. "Just in case."

"Never mind me!" shouted the captain, his alcohol-laden breath assaulting Cooper's nose.

"Are you drunk?" Cooper asked. "I can smell whiskey on your breath."

"Davis, we don't have time for this. We're going down."

"You should go up on deck," said Cooper. "You're in no state to help."

"Do as you're told," snarled the captain.

Cooper turned back into his room.

"There's a hole," Gavin whimpered. "I caught it on the nail you warned me about." He looked at Cooper, tears in his eyes. "My mother begged me to stay home. Said I'd die out here. She's right. I'm going to die, aren't I, Davis? I'm never going to see my mother again or Suzie. The whole reason I came on this stupid boat was for Suzie. I want to marry her."

Cooper rolled his eyes. "No one is going to die today. Not you and not me." He threw his suit at Gavin. "Put mine on."

Gavin shook his head. "I can't. I can't move."

"Yes, you can," said Cooper, helping Gavin slip his feet into the full suit. He pulled the kid up, shoved his hands into the arms, pulled the hood up, and zipped the suit as Gavin started to cry.

Cooper grabbed his chin. "You are not gonna die, Hart. Do you hear me? You are going up on deck and get that life boat ready. Then you're going to get in the damn boat, and you're going to live. The minute you get on land, you hug your Momma and kiss that girl. You hear me? And if you love her, don't ever leave her again."

Gavin nodded as Cooper pushed him out the door. "I expect to be in the lifeboat as soon as I get my suit on. I'm counting on you, Hart. We're all gonna make it."

The kid gave Cooper one more determined nod before running toward the stairs. Cooper turned and headed to the galley. The boat listed to port side, causing Cooper to tumble. His mind raced. He had to get Captain Mullis out.

Cooper struggled to make his way out of the room. Captain Mullis lay near the stairs, just where Cooper knew he'd be. His first thought was to leave him there. The drunk fool deserved to go down with the ship. He had endangered all their lives.

Water filled the galley as Cooper made his way to the Captain, who had taken Cooper's advice and was already in his survival suit.

"Captain Mullis, wake up!" yelled Cooper. The cold water felt like tiny shards of glass stabbing Cooper's socked feet as he pulled the Captain up the fun house stairs. Defying gravity, he made it to the top, just in time to see two more deck hands crawl out of the engine room, smoke billowing out behind them. Neither had on their Gumby suits.

The men pulled the captain the rest of the way out of the staircase, inflated his life vest, and threw him over the side of the boat.

The boat groaned at it tilted even more, threatening to completely capsize. "We have to swim for the lifeboat," said Cooper. "We need to go now, or we'll all die."

"Are you crazy?" said one of the men. "We'll die of hypothermia. Its better we stay on the boat. The Coast Guard is coming. We'll be safe here."

"Well, I'm going," said Cooper. "The ship is going to explode. We're all gonna end up in the water anyway. We need to save ourselves."

Then men grabbed him. "Davis, you've lost your mind. You have to stay here."

An explosion from the engine room rocked the ship again, causing the men to stumble. Cooper fell toward the water, this time letting himself fall, bracing himself for the impact of the cold sea. He hit the water, the cold causing him to lose his breath.

He tried to remain calm, tried to remember where the surface was. His fingers instantly went numb making it hard to swim, but he reached toward the light as hard as he could, breaking the surface just in time to see the boat sinking beneath the waves. The two deckhands were still clinging to fragments, trying to stay out of the water.

He tried to yell at them to get away from the boat, that the suction would take them down too, but he lacked the air and strength to get his message across. He couldn't help them now; he had to find the lifeboat. He had to make sure Gavin was okay. He had lived this time, too.

Twirling in a circle, he finally spotted the bright red boat. It was a good hundred yards away from him. He could just make out the Hart kid pulling Captain Mullis into the raft. "Good," he thought, "the kid made it to the raft."

He turned his focus on Sage. He had to get back to her. Mustering up all the strength he had left, he swam toward the boat. "I must get back to Sage" were his final words before his world went dark.

Cooper woke up in the barn and shivered. His clothes were dry, but the icy waters of the Bering Strait held on. *I have to find Sage,* he said staggering through the barn. *I have to see her.*

Focusing on Sage, as he had a million times over the past year, he appeared by her side. She lay in bed, tears streaming down her face.

"I told you not to go, Coop. I told you not to go," she chanted.

Cooper lay down facing her and gently caressed her hair. *I know you did, baby. I wish I would've listened to you. I tried like hell to stop it. I tried. I promise, I'll never go again.*

Chapter 22

"Is Lucas feeling better?" Becca asked, looking over the lake. "He seemed really shaken up yesterday. Ever find out what happened?"

Noah shook his head. "No, I found Cooper when I checked on Sage. I told Lucas as much, and when I asked Cooper what happened, he wouldn't talk about it."

"I've heard some people say spirits relive their deaths on the anniversary," said Becca.

"I hadn't heard that, or I would've warned him. No one should have to go through that twice," said Noah. He eyeballed his sister. "You're gonna have to tell him."

"I know." Becca rolled her eyes.

"Before you leave. It's not like you can call him. He's going to be looking for answers."

"Noah," Becca snapped, "I know I have to tell him. Back off."

Noah threw up his hands. "I just don't want to get stuck with him all upset at me because you didn't have the nerve to tell him before leaving."

"I'll go tell him now. Will that make you happy?"

"It will," said Noah.

She started walking toward Cooper who stood by the lake. Suddenly, she stopped and looked back at her brother. "Are you coming?"

He shrugged. "Am I supposed to?"

"Yes, he's your ghost."

Noah walked to his sister. "He is not my ghost."

"Well, he's sure not coming home with me."

Approaching Cooper, Becca cleared her throat so he'd know they were coming.

So you're tag teaming me. This can't be good. Cooper laughed. *But it'll still beat yesterday.*

"Where did you go yesterday?" asked Noah.

Doesn't matter, said Cooper, shaking his head. *Are you ready to talk to Sage for me? I have so much I need to say, especially after yesterday. Please, tell me you're going to help me.*

He looked right at Becca.

She hugged herself before starting. "Yesterday, when she remembered it was the anniversary of your death, she became very overwhelmed."

What do you mean "when she remembered"? Did she forget? Cooper crossed his arms. *She wouldn't forget.*

"You know how it is, Cooper," explained Noah. "We've been waking up and going full tilt trying to get this place ready for guests. I bet she didn't even look at the calendar. Remembering that day is the last thing she wants to think of."

"Not the point," said Becca. "She did remember, and it was hard on her."

I'm sure it was, said Cooper. *It was a rough day all around. That's why you need to tell her I'm here. She needs to know I haven't really gone anywhere.*

"And what do you think that will accomplish?" asked Becca.

Cooper shrugged. *Well, she won't have to be sad because I'm still here. Come on!* He kicked the ground. *This isn't that hard, people. I talk, then you talk. She smiles and knows I'm here for her, and we all live happily ever after.*

"I just don't see it going that way," said Becca. "Can I be honest with you?"

I wish you would. Cooper crossed his arms.

Becca sighed. "I was with her when she remembered. I saw her heartache and how much your death has affected her. Knowing you're still around will be a constant reminder of what she can never have - a long life with you. And having that constant reminder means she will never move into a relationship where she can actually love someone physically."

She doesn't need that kind of love as long as we have each other.

"I think we both know that isn't true," said Becca. "You've spent the last year loving someone you can't touch or even speak to. How has that made you feel?" Becca placed her hand on her heart. "I feel for you, Cooper. I really do. But I have to do what is best for Sage. I think Noah is right. I think she needs to continue believing you're gone so she can move on. Knowing you're here will bring her nothing but heartache."

I would never do anything to hurt Sage.

"Then listen to me, Cooper. I'm really trying to help," said Becca. "If I go in there and tell her you're still here, what do you think will happen next?"

We can go on as we always have, loving each other. She'll know she's not alone.

"You know as soon as I tell her, Noah's gone. He won't stick around to play mystic walkie-talkie. Once we've both left, you're right back where you started. You can't touch each other or have a conversation. She will never truly be happy, and she'll be lonelier than ever. Because even though you're here, you're not. And she will never move on with anyone else. Because if you don't go into the light, she'll never have true closure over losing you."

What is it with you Finnleys and the light? All Sage needs to know is that I'm here. Why is this so hard for you guys to understand?

"We understand just fine," said Noah. "Maybe even a little bit better than you since we are on the outside looking in. We're familiar with how this ends. It isn't pretty, Cooper."

You're far from being on the outside, Finnley. Cooper thrust his finger in Noah's face. *You've convinced your sister to stay silent for you because you want Sage for yourself. Did you tell her you kissed Sage? Does she know how you feel about her?*

"Cooper, I promise this has nothing to do with Noah," Becca interjected.

It has everything to do with him! Cooper shouted. *I've gone through hell and back to stay with Sage. I'll find a way to talk to her, even without your help. You won't keep us apart.*

And with that Cooper disappeared.

"Do you think he'll go to the girls?" asked Becca. "I'm not sure they'll keep their mouths shut. And if they don't, you might be moving in with us after all."

Noah shook his head. "I honestly don't know what Cooper will do next."

From the tree line, Cooper watched the girls fill the bird feeders with Lucas. He promised he'd stay away from the twins, but soon they would leave, and so would his opportunity to talk to Sage. He knew there was no way Noah was ever going to relay messages for him.

Lexi walked up beside him.

Shhh, devil dog, I don't want them to see me yet.

She backed into the shadows.

Cooper sighed. *I don't really want to involve the girls. They're so young, and this has to be scary for them. But I don't see that I have any other choice. They could be my last chance.*

He looked to Lexi. *Wouldn't you take the chance? I mean, I'm not out to do anything vicious. I just want to talk to Sage. Of course, Becca probably put some kind of voodoo on them. You'll never believe what she said. She thinks Sage is better off without me. That I should allow her to be in a physical relationship with someone else. The whole thought of it makes me sick.*

He leaned against a tree. *She's only protecting Noah by not talking to Sage for me. She wants to see the two of them together. Sure it's been hard to not be able to touch Sage, to hold her . . . to kiss her.* Cooper frowned. *Maybe Becca is right. Maybe that is too much to ask of Sage. I don't want to see her in the same kind of pain I've been in for the past year.*

With that thought, Cooper watched Becca call the girls to the van. They said their goodbyes to Lucas, Sage, and Noah and in less than ten minutes, Cooper's "last chance" drove out of Winter Song. His heart ached, but Becca had gotten to him. Was staying around really what was best for Sage, or was it best for him?

Chapter 23

It is amazing how much got accomplished when people were trying to avoid each other, Sage thought as she walked the length of the porch, touching the new banisters she had stained the day before. Her heart burst with pride as she looked around the grounds. Noah had done a wonderful job over the past month helping her get Winter Song fixed up. The place looked nothing like its former self.

Thinking of Noah, she sat on the swing. She could hear him hammering the finishing touches in the barn. He tried so hard to act normal with her after the kiss that happened a month ago. Actually, both of them had buried their heads into work.

Their days had been filled with casual encounters at meal times, starting each day with a hearty breakfast and an agenda for the day's to-do list. Most of the time, Noah came in and grabbed a quick sandwich for lunch, taking it with him as he gazed at the lake. Dinner was filled with an awkward recap of all the chores done for the day before Noah excused himself to work on the barn. It was an endless routine of avoidance, but every once in a while, she'd catch him staring at her with a tiny smile. A smile that made her heart melt. A smile she couldn't help but return.

The hammering stopped, bringing Sage's attention to the barn door. Noah walked out of the barn, beads of sweat dripping off his forehead and sliding down his shirtless chest. Sage bit her lip as she watched him down a full glass of ice tea.

This is foolish, Sage thought, walking toward him. Winter Song would open soon, and the guests didn't need to feel the tension between the partners. She appreciated a hard-working man. No need to be embarrassed or act like a school girl with a crush on the quarterback. She was an adult, and she would make this work.

"How's it coming along?" she asked, shading her eyes from the sun. It was an unusually hot day for May.

Noah pulled a bandanna out of his back pocket and wiped his brow. "Come on in and take a look."

Just no funny business, like the last time y'all were in here, Cooper sneered, appearing behind Sage. He had not left her side since the kiss. *She's made her feelings towards you very clear.*

Sage walked in and waited for her eyes to adjust. A cement slab gave way to beautiful cherry floors which led to a small kitchenette paralleled by a cozy living area. Just behind the living room, she saw a door she knew led to a small bathroom, equipped with its own shower. Up the short stairway to the loft stood a full-size bed flanked on one side by a glorious handmade bookcase with a fold out desk and on the other side, a matching chest of drawers. The pocket privacy screen was pulled out just enough for Sage to see how it could be wheeled all the way to the stairs, giving the bedroom occupant privacy. Noah thought of everything.

"It's breathtaking," she said.

Cooper shrugged. *I could've done better.*

Sage traced the cement countertops. "I would've never thought cement countertops would look so great. I guess if we overbook, we can always put a guest out here."

"As long as they don't mind sleeping with the cars." Noah laughed. "Besides, where would I sleep?"

"We'll pitch you a tent." She winked at Noah. "You're not really going to put the cars in here, right?" Sage raised an eyebrow. "That can't be safe sleeping with all that exhaust in the air."

Oh, let's let him try. Cooper smiled at Noah.

"Only if the weather merits it," Noah flipped a switch causing two big fans on the ceiling to circulate. "I just finished installing the breaker to the exhaust fans. You could leave a car running in here and never suffocate." He flipped the switch off. "Though, I don't recommend trying it."

Ahh, come on, Cooper pleaded. *Just once?*

"I don't remember industrial exhaust fans being in the budget." Sage wondered just how much of a tab Noah had run up at the hardware store.

"They weren't on the budget." Noah placed his hand on the doorjamb. "I paid for them."

I thought you were broke? Cooper ran his hands together. *Looks like you just got caught in a lie.*

"I wish you wouldn't have done that," said Sage. "There's no way you could afford these on your own, and I can't afford to pay you back."

"Oh, I can think of other ways for you to pay me back," Noah teased, then cried out as the door slammed on his fingers and bounced back open.

"Oh, my God," Sage said running toward Noah. "What happened? Are you okay?"

I told you not to test me, didn't I, Finnley? Cooper stood behind the door and glared at Noah.

"Wind must've blown the door shut," said Noah, grimacing. "It was my own fault for leaving my hand there." He looked at his fingers and struggled to bend them. All five bent. "I don't think anything's broken." He glared back at Cooper. "I'll be fine."

"What I was saying was . . . ," Noah took a deep breath. ". . . you can pay me back by giving me a couple of days off next week to go fishing with my buddy, Carl. He gave me the exhaust fans as payment for some work I did for him about a year ago on the old Flinn garage. Flinn wouldn't pay for the fans even after promising Carl to reimburse him. So Carl repo'd the fans. I thought it was a good trade. Carl said they were just collecting dust at his place, going to waste. He came out with his crane and helped me put them in place a few days ago while you were in town, so I promised him a fishing trip."

Of course, that's what you meant, time off to fish. Yeah, right, mocked Cooper.

"I'm sure some time off can be arranged," said Sage. "You've worked really hard to get this place into shape. I'm amazed at what you've done in such a short amount of time. I can't tell you how much I appreciate it. There's no way I could've done it without you."

"Oh, there's still a lot to do," said Noah, looking at his fingers as he flexed them up and down. "I'm gonna go work on that leaky pipe under the upstairs sink, now that the barn's done. I'll be moving in here tonight, so we can start on that room tomorrow, if that's all right with you."

Sage shrugged. "That was our agreement."

What did you expect her to say? That you could just move into her room?

Noah turned to head toward the house.

"Noah," Sage called out.

He turned. "Yeah?"

"I didn't just come out here to look at the barn, though I'm not sure we can call it the barn anymore."

"Okay," said Noah, facing her.

"It's just that," Sage bit her fingernail. "Well, I've just felt we've been a little off, since. . ."

"Off?" Noah rubbed the back of his neck. "Not sure I'm following."

"Don't tell me you haven't noticed."

"Sage, I really don't know what you're talking about. If you feel my work isn't up to par, then just tell me, and I'll fix it."

"No, your work is great. I've already said that."

"Then what?" asked Noah.

"It's nothing. I'm just being silly."

Noah nodded at Sage and walked toward the house, still flexing his hand. Sage watched him walk away without the air being cleared as she had wanted to do. It wasn't as if she felt he was mad at her, but he didn't seem like the same easygoing Noah. She hardly ever heard him talk to himself anymore. Maybe she should take a cue from him and continue to act like everything was okay? Maybe "clearing the air" was only gonna muck it up?

What in the world are you thinking about? Cooper asked Sage. *I know that look, and it's never good.*

Grabbing his tool belt from the porch, Noah took one last look over his shoulder before heading into the house. Sage was still in the barn, apparently with Cooper, who was getting stronger every day. It wouldn't be long before Sage would figure out on her own that Cooper was still here.

Chapter 24

Noah's torso was shoved under the small vanity in the upstairs bathroom when Cooper found him.

I told you to back off from Sage, Cooper growled. *You were flirting with her.*

"I didn't do anything but make a statement that you took inappropriately," Noah said from beneath the sink, "and that sounds like a personal problem."

We both know what you meant.

Noah slid himself out and looked at Cooper. "Honestly, I didn't mean anything by it. But I'm not going anywhere. Can't you see that? Sage is used to having me around, just as she's used to the fact that you're gone, forever. It's only a matter of time before she chooses a life of real love, instead of a memory. I'm not trying to disrespect what you two had, but it's over. It will never be as it was. If you truly loved her, you'd go into the stupid light and let her be happy."

Again, happy with you. Cooper let out a short laugh. *I'm not gonna fall for your lies. You may have Sage and the ol' man fooled, but I know the kind of man you are, and you don't get to be with Sage.*

"Oh yeah?" Noah narrowed his eyes. "And just what kind of man is that? You've called me everything from a con man to a hack who couldn't complete the job. I've been here for months, and I haven't taken advantage of Sage in any way. Every job she's asked me to do, I've done and done well."

You're a womanizer. Cooper crossed his arms.

"How so? Sage asked me to give her space, and I've done it. But she'll come back to me. You can't stop this."

Then you need to leave. If you don't on your own, I'll make you so miserable you'll want to leave.

Noah shook his head and slid back under the vanity. "I'm not scared of you. You're just upset because you know Sage will pick me over the memory of you."

I will not let you live my life!

Cooper's face grew hot as he stared at the pipe Noah was fixing. The pipe groaned once and then burst causing rusty, muddy water to shower Noah's face. Noah cursed, scuttled out, and turned off the main water valve.

He looked at Cooper, the earthy musk smell of fresh dirt and copper filling his nostrils. Grabbing a towel, he quickly dried his face. "Pipes burst all the time, especially in old houses."

Keep believin' that, pal. Cooper laughed. *We both know who made that happen. And that's not the only thing I can do. I'm getting stronger every day, and it won't be long before I can literally haul your sorry ass off this property.*

Cooper had never felt so much power. After bursting the light when Noah kissed Sage, he felt drained. That was not the case now as energy coursed through his veins. He took delight in watching Noah mop the floor with an old towel, his hair flaked with mud and bits of rust.

Noah took off his boots, grabbed the duffle bag of clothes he had packed earlier, and made his way downstairs as Cooper followed.

Sage took one look at him and laughed. "What happened to you?"

"Pipe burst." Noah rubbed the back of his neck. "I'm going to take a shower, then run into town to get a replacement. Don't use the water upstairs."

"What's with all the rust and mud?" she asked, trying not to laugh. "Is there a problem with the well?"

"Just build up in the old pipes, I think. Since we haven't seen rusty or dirty water anywhere else in the house, I'm not sure exactly what to make of it. Just keep an eye on things. If the water starts to look funny, we'll get someone with more plumbing experience to take a look. Until then, I think we'll just call it a fluke." He glanced at Cooper. "I'm going to the barn to shower."

I knew you didn't think it was an ordinary pipe burst, bragged Cooper following Noah to the barn. *Are you going to leave her alone now? Possibly go into town for 'a part' and never return? Cause that would be super.*

"All I know is the wind blew the door shut on my fingers, the old pipes gave out upstairs, and Sage kissed me back," said Noah, slamming the bathroom door in Cooper's face.

Cooper paced the barn. Finnley wasn't learning his lesson. Why was he willing to compete with years of true love? Because Cooper was dead, that's why, and Noah had no respect. Cooper stared at the steam flowing under the bathroom door and made his way to the hot water heater. Kneeling he concentrated on the pilot. The light flickered and then grew until there was an orange hot flame making Noah's shower water boiling hot.

A few minutes later, he heard Noah's yelp and curse as the water turned off.

"For the love of . . ., Cooper," yelled Noah, barreling out of the bathroom with a towel wrapped around his waist. "What did you do now?"

Cooper shrugged. *I didn't do anything. Remember I can't do anything . . . I'm dead.*

"I know you did something." Noah made his way to the hot water heater. "It's a brand new tank. The only reason the water would get that hot . . ." He bent down and looked at the pilot.

Tinkering with the knobs, Noah tried to find the problem. Finding nothing, he rose. "Doesn't matter, I was done anyway."

Noah grabbed the duffle out of the bathroom and headed up to the loft. He glanced at Cooper. "A little privacy, please?"

Not on your life, pal, said Cooper. *I want you to know that every time you want to get intimate with Sage, I'm gonna be there.*

"Pervert," Noah mumbled.

Think what you want. Cooper snickered. *But I can't imagine all your 'plumbing' will work with you knowing I'm there. You just don't seem like the type that likes an audience.*

Noah finished getting dressed and headed to his truck. Cooper followed.

"Seriously?" Noah whirled around.

You have two choices, pal. Relay my messages to Sage and leave her alone, or you won't have a moment of peace. Cooper poked his finger at Noah's chest. *I'm gonna be there, and remember, I don't sleep.*

"Well, come on then," said Noah. "I've got to go to town."

Noah hopped in the truck, and Cooper sat next to him.

"You're going to get mighty bored hanging out with me all day," said Noah. "Why don't you spend this time making peace with your father and moving into the light?"

You sound like a broken record. Cooper rolled his eyes. *You can stop with the whole "go into the light" thing. It ain't gonna happen unless Sage is by my side.*

"As long as you're hanging out with me," said Noah, "then you're going to hear about two things: your dad and going into the light. How'd Lucas end up in the wheelchair?"

How would I know? said Cooper. *Why can't you find a woman that's not already taken?*

Noah smiled at Cooper as he parked in front of the hardware store. "As far as I can tell, she's not."

Cooper watched as Noah got out of the car and started rummaging through the odds and ends sitting in front of the hardware store for their annual sidewalk sale. Nestled in the corner eve of the store sat a sparrow's nest, complete with mother sparrow and two chicks.

Cooper grinned as he approached the nest. The sparrow eyed him suspiciously until he was too close for her comfort. The bird swooped through him. Cooper ran towards Noah, and the bird focused all her energy on the one human she could actually hit.

"What the . . . ?" Noah yelled, trying to dodge the bird's attack.

Duck and cover! Cooper yelled laughing. *Duck and cover!*

Noah ran up and down the sidewalk, his hands trying to protect his head and face at the same time.

Maybe you should stop, drop, and roll. Cooper continued to laugh.

Noah finally managed to get inside the hardware store without the bird following him. The customers all stared. Cooper leaned into Noah's shoulder. *I may be dead, but I am far from harmless.*

Chapter 25

Sage watched Noah drive into town, then stared at the last two boxes in her closet. That was it. They were all that was left to be unpacked. Once those two boxes were empty, her transition would be complete, and her "new life" could begin.

She sighed and whispered, "New life."

What exactly did that mean? She was opening her own business and living in a new house, but was she really ready to begin a "new life"? Especially one without Cooper? Maybe one with Noah?

She shook the thoughts away. It was time to get to work, not contemplate the meaning of life. Contemplating the meaning of life was better done in the wee hours of the night when she couldn't sleep. When no one could see her tears or hear her sobs. When she could talk to Cooper and not feel like a fool.

She pulled out the first box. Taking her keys out of her pocket, she slid them through the tape, breaking the seal. Pillows, trapped for months in the small box, billowed up at her. So that's where all my throw pillows are, she thought with a giggle. This box is going to be easy breezy. But the box was a little heavy for just pillows. There had to be something on the bottom.

She grabbed the pillows out and set them on the bed beside her. Gasping, she pulled out the scrapbook that sat at the bottom of the box. It was the very scrapbook she had been working on when Richard came to tell her that Cooper was . . . well, gone.

She shook her head no. "This is not the time to think about that," she said to herself. "It's time to unpack this box and move on to the next one. Just put the book on the shelf and move on. There's no need to walk down memory lane. Lots of stuff to do."

As she pulled the album out of the box, a couple of pictures fluttered to the ground. Cooper's face, surrounded with wildflowers, stared up at her. She tried to swallow her tears, tried to put the memory of that night in the far reaches of her mind, but it didn't work.

Leaning against the foot of her bed, she stared at the photo. "I told you not to go," she said softly as the tears took over and her memory turned to the day the photo was taken. She remembered that day as if it were just last week.

"Will you put the camera down?" Cooper whined after Sage had taken the shot. "If I would've known I was going to be the subject of a photo shoot, I would've taken more time to look GQ for you."

Sage sat on the blanket beside Cooper. "You always look GQ to me, baby. I want you to be the subject of every photo shoot from now until forever."

"Forever is a long time," said Cooper.

"You think?" Sage tilted her head.

Cooper nodded. "It is, but forever isn't long enough."

"Long enough for what?" asked Sage, taking a bite of her picnic sandwich.

"To love you." Cooper slid a piece of Sage's hair behind her ear. "I need more time than that."

Sage smiled. "Okay, I'll give you forever and one day, but nothing more. After that it's over, pal."

"Well, if that's all I get I better take advantage now." A wicked smile crossed Cooper's face before he devoured her in a kiss. Sage dropped her sandwich and kissed him back, rolling onto her back to feel his full weight on top of her. As he kissed her neck, Sage looked at the sky and thanked God for giving her Cooper.

Sage slapped her hand on her forehead, trying to dislodge the memory. But it was too late, she was sobbing as if she had just found out about his death. There was no holding back the grief. The anniversary of his death still hung heavy in the air. She slid down against the bed and let the tears take over, thankful Noah was in town. If he were here, he'd try to comfort her, and being in the arms of another man would only make her feel worse. Or would it?

Lucas wheeled himself into the room, causing Sage to quickly dry her eyes. She looked up at him as he came close enough to see at the picture.

"That's a good picture," he said. "It catches his essence. He always did have a good aura. I can see why it makes you cry."

"It's been a while since I've cried like this," Sage admitted. "I know it seems foolish, but sometimes I just have to have a moment."

"I've had many a moment since my Maggie passed. She was a good woman and deserved a better man than an old drunk like me. There is much I would like to say to her." Lucas sighed. "She is one of my many regrets, as is Cooper."

"So why did Cooper say you were de...?" Sage couldn't finish the question.

Lucas looked at his hands. "I beat Cooper's mom half to death in a drunken rage. When I woke up from my binge, I couldn't remember anything. I looked down and saw bloody hands but knew it wasn't my blood. There was no doubt I had done something terrible. When I couldn't find Maggie or Cooper in the house, I knew I had done something to her. Once I found out she was in the hospital, I ran just like a coward. I couldn't even look at her, much less apologize. So I just left. I never loved anyone like I loved her and my son. So I did the best thing for them at the time, I disappeared. It was the only way I could guarantee I would never be the one to hurt them again."

"You beat Maggie?" Sage's eyes grew wide.

Lucas gave his head a sad nod. "I was in a dark place. The demons of alcohol and depression had their grip on me and I couldn't shake them. I wanted to take it back, but there is no going back from that. I hated myself."

"Cooper never said a word," Sage whispered. "I had no idea."

"I think it was easier on him to think of me as dead. It was good that I left. Gave them time to move on with their lives."

"Where did you go?" asked Sage.

"No place in particular," answered Lucas. "I went wherever I could go to get cheap booze. Spent a lot of nights in the drunk tank. Then one day I woke up in

Statehaven. That's when I planned on taking my own life. What good was I to anyone? So I started stealing people's medications, hiding them in the wall until I thought I had enough to kill myself. No one would care about an old drunk overdosing."

He turned the wheelchair to look out the window and continued. "That last day in Statehaven, I counted 56 pills, and even though I didn't know what half of them were, I figured it was enough. All I had to do was wait until lights out. I wrote Maggie a letter, telling her how sorry I was and that I'd do my penance in the afterlife so we could be together. That was the day Cooper came and got me. It was the day I found out my beloved Maggie was gone. That was the day I found out that even on her deathbed, she still believed in me."

"You ruined her, you know," said Sage, trying to control the anger in her voice.

He turned back to face Sage. "I did not know that until Cooper came to get me. But even after he told me, I had this funny notion that Cooper would come and visit me in Pleasant Valley. I got sober, refused medicine of any kind. I wanted a clear head so I could apologize and have a relationship with my son. I was mean to everyone, refusing to speak to anyone but Cooper. I thought they would call him and tell him I had to leave. Then they told me he died. One of the nurses saw his picture on the news, or I would've never known. My chance was gone."

"At that moment, I once again, planned on taking my own life." He rubbed his hands on the arms of the wheelchair. "Then you brought me here, and I can feel Cooper's presence in you. So I've decided to live. I've decided to make my amends to you, since I can no longer make them with my son."

"I don't know how to take all this," said Sage. "I saw how your actions affected Cooper and his mother."

"I will understand if you want me to leave, but I hope you would allow me to try to make up for my mistakes. I am not the same person I was before." Lucas folded his hands in his lap.

Sage looked down at the picture of Cooper. Maggie's last request of her son had been to make sure Lucas was taken care of. Sage would honor that request since Cooper couldn't.

She looked up. "You can stay, but I have one condition . . ."

"Name it," said Lucas.

"That you stop using that wheelchair. I've seen you walking in your room. I know it's a lie, and if you're going to make amends, then you can't lie to me."

Lucas set the parking brake and stood. "You're right. No more lies."

Chapter 26

The butterflies in Sage's belly did somersaults as she watched the black sedan pull into the drive. They did it. Just a short four weeks after Becca and the girls left, Sage was watching her first guests pull into Winter Song. Her dream was coming true, and being booked solid on her opening weekend was not only thrilling, but terrifying.

Noah patted her hand twice. "It's going to be great," he assured her. "No need to worry. You've thought of everything."

I agree, said Cooper, grinning at Sage who glowed with excitement. *You've made our dream come true. I'm so proud of you.*

"You think?" asked Sage, looking at Noah.

"I know so," said Noah, "and I think Cooper would be proud of what you've done here."

"I think so too." Sage managed a small smile, tears welling up at the thought of Cooper not being around to experience their first guests at Winter Song.

Sage blinked back the tears and plastered on her most sincere smile as the couple exited the car. She approached the woman as Noah went to help the man with the luggage.

"Welcome to Winter Song," Sage said, shaking the woman's hand. "We're so pleased you've come. You must be Patricia Evans."

"Please call me Tricia. Patricia is my mother," Mrs. Evans said looking around, her blond ponytail swinging in unison. "What a beautiful place. Oh, Phil, this is going to be great." She looked back at Sage. "We're celebrating our fifth wedding anniversary. Feels like we've been married for ages but haven't seen each other in a decade . . . If you know what I mean."

"Happy anniversary," said Sage. "We've put you in the Grizzly Room. It's our best room. It has a wonderful view of the lake and its own private balcony. Great for 'seeing' one another again."

"Lovely," said Tricia, gold bracelets jingling together as she placed her hands on her hips. "I can't wait to explore this place."

Sage led the Evanses up to their room. She couldn't help but burst with pride as Tricia kept repeating the word "lovely" with every corner they turned. She noticed Phil didn't say a word until he heard the evening menu of chicken cordon bleu, grilled wild asparagus with hollandaise sauce, and roasted sweet potatoes, followed by fresh apple pie. "Now, that sounds lovely," he said rubbing his belly.

Within the next hour the other two couples, the Collinses and the Jenkinses, arrived, and Winter Song was officially full on its opening weekend. Sage hummed to herself as she started the prep work for the dinner.

That Evans woman is right, you know, Cooper said, sliding his hands around Sage's waste without really touching her. It was the closest he could come to actually hugging her. *The place is lovely.*

Tricia slid onto a barstool, catching Sage completely off guard. This was why she had the open kitchen, but she figured the guests were taking in the sights of the property or getting settled.

"I can't believe you left the kitchen open," said Tricia. "If people saw the way I cook, they'd run out the door screaming."

Not my woman. Cooper smiled. *They wouldn't be able to take their eyes off her to notice the mess.*

Sage shrugged. "I like my guests to feel at home since I only have three rooms to fill. Plus, what chef wants to be cooped up in the kitchen when all the fun is being had in the dining and living areas?"

"My mother always said the same thing. Without fail, my entire family ends up in the kitchen during the holidays. The women to help, the men to graze." Tricia giggled as she helped herself to a cherry tomato.

Sage joined in with Tricia's giggle as the bell jingled above the door. Sage looked up and saw Richard standing behind a huge bouquet of spring flowers.

"Richard," squealed Sage, "it's been too long. Where have you been hiding?"

He sat the bouquet on the bar and gave Sage a quick hug as Cooper moved out of the way. "You know the law never sleeps. These are for you." He pointed to the flowers. "You've done an amazing job on the place."

That's what I keep saying, said Cooper.

"Hasn't she though?" said Tricia. "It's absolutely lovely."

Sage slapped her forehead. "Where are my manners? Richard this is our very first guest, Tricia Evans. Tricia, this is Deputy Richard Park."

"Nice to meet you," Richard gave Tricia's hand a quick shake. "Did a special occasion bring you to Winter Song, Miss Evans?"

Cooper chuckled. *Always the nosey cop.*

"Mrs. Evans, but you can call me Tricia. My husband and I are celebrating our anniversary, but I'm also a writer. I'm always looking for inspiration, and I believe I'll find plenty of inspiration at this particular B&B. My husband, Phil, is upstairs talking architecture with Sage's husband."

Sage's what? Cooper squawked. *That two bit hack is not Sage's husband. Why would you even think that?*

"Husband?" Richard raised his eyebrows at Sage. "Did my invitation get lost in the mail?"

Sage tried to swallow her giggle, but it came out sounding more like a startled cat. She looked at Tricia. "There's been a misunderstanding. Noah's not my husband."

Damn right he's not. She's far too good for him.

Tricia's cheeks flushed red. "Oh, I'm so sorry. I figured you were married and ran the place together."

Cooper walked toward Tricia. *She'd never marry a low life like that.*

Sage shook her head. "No, we're just business partners. I'm lucky to have him. He's great with a hammer."

"I bet that's not all he's good at," Tricia said under her breath. "If I weren't married, I'd swoop Noah up in a heartbeat. What a piece of man candy."

Gross, said Cooper.

Sage shrugged. "I hadn't noticed, but I couldn't have gotten this place ready without him."

Tricia slapped Sage playfully on the arm. "Girl, you'd have to be blind not to notice."

Richard cleared his throat. "Well, as much as I'm not enjoying this conversation, I better be getting back to town before y'all start painting my fingernails. I'll see you later, Sage. Let's do lunch sometime when you're not busy. There's something I need to talk to you about. Something important."

Cooper raised his eyebrows. *Crap, not you too.*

"Oh, don't let me keep you," said Tricia, "if it's important."

Richard raised his hand. "Not important as in urgent, just important in a personal way."

For the love of . . . are there no other single ladies in this town? asked Cooper.

"Well, if you're sure you don't want to talk now." Sage paused giving Richard a chance to change his mind. "We'll do lunch next week. I'm sure I can make that happen. Okay?"

Or you could just forget about it all together. We all know what he's gonna say. Cooper chimed in following Richard to the front door. *I'll see you out. I'd like to have a little chat.*

As Richard left, a mischievous smile rose on Tricia's face. "I think he likes you."

"It's not like that. We've been friends forever," Sage explained as she snapped the asparagus.

Noah and Phil came into the kitchen and made their way to the bar.

"You've got yourself one hell of a carpenter," said Phil. "I might have to steal him when we do our deck next year."

"That is if you can spare him." Tricia winked at Sage.

"She does just fine on her own," said Noah. "This girl took on a full sow grizzly guarding a carcass this winter."

"With the help of the dog," Sage interjected.

"Ah, she's just being modest. She's pretty special." Noah gazed at Sage, causing a snort-laugh to explode from Tricia.

The three stared at Tricia.

"I think we missed the joke," Noah said to Phil. "Come on. I'll show you the converted barn."

Phil gave a quizzical look to his wife and then followed Noah out the front door.

"What was so funny?" asked Sage.

"Girl, I may have to rent your room for the summer. I have a feeling what's going to happen here between the three of you would make a fantastic story."

Sage raised an eyebrow. "The three of us?"

"Yes." Tricia gestured to the door, "You, Mr. Lawman, and the hunky carpenter. If that doesn't have romance novel written all over it, I don't know what does."

Sage just shook her head as she grabbed the sweet potatoes from the pantry. Of course, she was aware of the tension between Noah and her, but Richard? Richard had been her friend for ages. He had been Coop's friend. There's no way he was interested in anything romantic. He knew the strong bond between her and Cooper. He wouldn't try to compete with that.

Sage glanced at the flowers, a mix of spring blooms with a single red rose in the middle. The single rose stood out like a hotel sign on a dark deserted highway, welcoming, but with a hint of apprehension.

She pushed the thought away. The rose was added for a pop of color, nothing else. Tricia was a writer; of course her imagination would see things that weren't there. Or was it that she saw things others didn't?

Chapter 27

Sage fidgeted with her napkin as she waited for Richard to show up for their lunch date. She felt badly leaving her guests alone for the afternoon to meet him, but Noah had taken the ladies on a nature hike while Lucas taught the men fly fishing, so it was the perfect opportunity for Sage to run to the store and meet with Richard for a late lunch.

Truth was Tricia's suspicions about Richard had left a bad taste in Sage's mouth. What if he was interested in her beyond their friendship? There was no waiting until next week to find out if Richard liked her that way. She needed to know, now.

Sage shook her head. It had to be something else. Richard had always been her friend, nothing more. Besides she had enough on her plate trying to deal with her feelings for Noah. She thought about their encounter that morning as Noah packed up a picnic lunch for the ladies going hiking.

"Are you sure you're up for this?" Sage asked. "I could always let Richard know I'm just too busy to do lunch right now. I'm sure he'll understand."

Noah tilted his head up. "If I remember correctly, the last time you went hiking in the woods you were almost eaten by a bear. I think it'd be safer for all of us for you to go into town."

"You can stop bringing that up now." Sage rolled her eyes. "You know darn well I can handle myself. I'm just not sure you can handle being around all those ladies who ogle you like you're the last piece of chocolate on the planet."

Noah leaned into Sage. "You know, I seem to remember a moment when you devoured me like I was the last piece of chocolate."

His words rolled over her like hot fudge covering vanilla ice cream on a steamy day. She glanced at his lips, licking hers, then leaned in. They were inches from each other when one of the shelves came crashing off the wall, causing Tricia and other guests to run down the stairs to make sure everything was all right.

Sage heard Noah mutter something under his breath as he retreated to fix the shelf and pick up the mess. She thought she heard the words, "Cooper" and "stupid light," but was sure her mind was playing tricks on her, her heart still racing from their almost second kiss.

The chair across from her slid out causing Sage to jump a little before looking up and smiling. "Richard, I'm glad you could make it. I was getting worried you had forgotten."

"No place I'd rather be. Just stuck at work," he said opening the menu. "I'm starved, had to skip breakfast on account of Mr. Cripter's bull in Mr. Snogging's garden. A bunch of nonsense."

Sage swallowed a giggle. "Guess there's nothing worse than waking up to a bull eating your prize cabbage. Good thing we've got a mighty officer such as yourself to keep the peace."

"Go ahead and laugh," said Richard, putting the menu down. "I was ready to shoot the stupid bull. I get called out on this petty crap all the time. Feels like I'm living in Mayberry. I guess I'm lucky they let me have more than one bullet."

"Ah, come on. It's gotta be better than being a cop in the city," said Sage, ". . . never knowing what danger lies around the corner."

"A little danger would be nice," said Richard. "Yesterday, Nicole Meeker came running into the station crying something awful. I jumped up, grabbing my gun, I just knew someone was chasing her with a machete or something."

"What was wrong with her?" asked Sage. "I hope she's okay."

"Someone stole her garden gnome."

Sage tried not to laugh. "Her gnome?"

Richard nodded. "Yep, someone came into her flower bed and stole her gnome named Norman."

"You're kidding," gasped Sage.

"Nope, even gave me a full description. Tall pointy hat, white beard, carrying a large grey goose."

"So did you find Norman?" Sage gave Richard an ornery smile.

"You're eating this up, aren't you?"

"You didn't answer the question, Officer."

"Of course I found him. I'm a damn good cop, and it didn't even take a damn good cop to know he was at the high school. The boys baseball team thought he'd make a good mascot." He smiled back at Sage.

"So you're the hero," said Sage.

"I'm nothing better than a rent-a-cop."

"Richard, don't say that. This community is lucky to have you. I don't know what we'd do without a good cop who's willing to track down garden gnomes. It's nice we all have someone who won't trivialize what each of us finds important."

"Well, that's kind of what I wanted to talk to you about," said Richard, before holding up a hand as the waitress stopped by. "I'll have the chicken fried steak, baked potato, and a salad with ranch."

The waitress looked at Sage who ordered a chicken salad sandwich and fries. Once the waitress left with their order, Richard continued. "I've got something in the works. Something big that will give me the life I've always wanted."

"Good for you, Richard," said Sage, smiling. "What is it? I want to hear all about it."

"Thing is, I can't stay here for it to work."

Sage lost her smile. "So you're moving?"

"If things work out like I hope they do, then yes. I can't stay here anymore. This place is draining the life out of me."

Sage straightened up and plastered her smile back on. "Well, I want nothing more than for you to be happy, and if moving away from here is what it takes, then I'm delighted for you. I'm not gonna lie, though, I'll miss you. We've been friends forever, I'm not gonna know what to do with myself without you around." She took a drink of her water, trying to wash down the lump that grew in her throat.

"Come with me."

Sage gasped, causing the water to go down the wrong pipe, sending her into a coughing fit.

"What?" she said, grabbing her napkin.

"If what I'm planning works out, I'll have enough money for us both to live comfortably for a long time, and I couldn't think of a better person to have by my side than you," Richard explained. "What do you say? Will you come with me?"

"I can't, Richard. You know I just opened Winter Song. I can't just up and leave it."

"I'm sure that carpenter and Cooper's father can run it just fine without you." Richard leaned back in his chair.

"Richard," Sage said softly, "I don't want them to handle it without me. I want to be there. This is my dream. You can't ask me to give that up."

Richard grabbed her hand. "Sage, I'm going to be honest with you. You've been more than a friend to me for a long time. Even before Coop died. I need us to be together. You need to come with me." He tightened his grip.

The waitress came with the food, giving Sage the opportunity to jerk her hand away. She gave the waitress an apologetic look. "Would you mind wrapping this up for me? I'm sorry, but I have to go."

The waitress nodded and took Sage's food away.

"Don't go, Sage," Richard pleaded. "Just think about what I'm offering you. You'd never have to work another day in your life. We could travel the world. See all the places you've dreamed about. You can't do that by staying here. You'll be stuck at Winter Song for the rest of your life."

The waitress came back with the to-go box, and Sage stood. "Since Coop died, I've only had one dream, Richard. And that was to make Winter Song happen in his memory. I don't care if I'm stuck there for the rest of my life. I want to be there. And you, being my oldest and dearest friend, should've known there would be only one answer to your asking me to leave."

Sage grabbed her purse and gave him a small smile. "I hope that when the time comes for you to leave, you will come out to Winter Song and tell me good-bye."

Richard grabbed her hand again. "Sage, it doesn't have to be good-bye. We can get you another B&B. Please, come with me."

Sage squeezed his hand. "I meant what I said when I said I want you to be happy. I just wish you felt the same way for me."

With that, she let go and walked away. She didn't know what hurt more, knowing her friend was moving away or the fact Richard wanted her to give up her dream for his.

Chapter 28

Sage sank into the oversized recliner after waving a final good-bye to Tricia and Phil Evans. She and Tricia had developed into friends over the weekend, and she was thankful Tricia had left her e-mail address. Of course, Sage had to promise to keep her up to date on all the torrid activity between Richard, Noah, and herself. Sage assured Tricia that her e-mails would be very boring. Especially after the lunch date between her and Richard.

She sighed and tried to will herself out of the comfy chair. She had two days to get ready for the next set of guests, unless she had a walk-in which didn't typically happen at B&B's. She knew though, if she didn't change the beds, scrub the bathrooms, and wash the linens, sure enough someone would come in looking for a place to stay and leave her scrambling. Not only did she need to take care of the rooms, but the menu for the next week also needed to be finalized, and probably a trip to the store was in order.

Sage rubbed her temples at the thought of the to-do list. A pair of rough, but tender hands began to rub her shoulders and without thinking Sage leaned into them.

"I'll give you ten minutes to stop that," she teased.

I'll give you thirty seconds, Cooper narrowed his eyes at Noah. *Haven't you learned your lesson yet, Finnley?*

Noah laughed. "You deserve every minute. You did a wonderful job this weekend. The food was fantastic, and everyone left happy. Not one complaint."

I've got a complaint, said Cooper. *You see there's a certain handyman that works at Winter Song that can't seem to keep his hands to himself.*

"Yes, it did go rather smoothly," Sage replied. "I have to admit I kept waiting for the other shoe to drop. I just knew I'd burn the food, mix up a reservation, or someone would find a squirrel in their closet."

"A squirrel in the closet, huh?" Noah laughed.

"You never know; it could happen." Sage laughed back. She liked the way his hands felt on her, the way they made lightning tingle through her body. She grabbed Noah's hand and led him in front of her. He kneeled to meet her gaze.

What are you doing, woman? For the love of God, I'm right here.

"I couldn't have done it without you," she said. "I was so afraid you were going to leave after our kiss. I should've handled that better."

You shouldn't have to handle it at all. It shouldn't have happened, Cooper snarled as he headed to the door. *I can't take this. If you're going to get all "Noah is the best thing since sliced bread," I'm outta here before I make something explode.*

"I understand this is a conflicted time for you," said Noah. "It can't be easy trying to move forward while living a dream you created with someone you loved very much."

"That's just it, Noah. Am I moving forward?" Sage asked. "I feel like I'm taking the steps, but am I actually getting anywhere? It's like being on a treadmill watching the nature channel. The only thing that's changing is the view."

"It wouldn't be fair for me to answer that question," said Noah.

"Why? I value your opinion." Sage tilted her head.

"Because . . . ," Noah looked around the room. "Because you know how I feel about you. My answer to your question would be biased."

"Do I?" asked Sage. "Do I really know how you feel about me? We shared an amazing kiss, and the other day we almost shared another. But that's it. You seem to respect me as a person, as your boss. But other than that I'm really not su . . ."

"I have fallen in love with you," he cut her off. "I don't know when it happened exactly. I just know it did."

Sage stared at him as he held up his hands.

"I know it sounds lame," he continued. "Just hear me out."

Sage nodded for him to continue.

"I have watched you put your heart and soul into this place. I've seen you open your home to a stranger because he's Cooper's family. Hell, you even opened your home to me, and all you knew about me was I had some skill with a hammer and was being evicted. You have the biggest heart and a glow about you that's contagious. I understand Cooper was the love of your life, and I'm not trying to take his place. I just hope there is room in your heart for another love. Even if that person isn't me. I just want you to be happy and will do everything in my power to make you that way, no matter how long it takes."

Sage leaned forward. She intended to place her hand on his shoulder and let him down easy. She intended to fire him for his own good, to set him free to find someone who could love him back. But instead she found herself running her hands through his soft hair as she straddled herself over his knees and kissed him gently.

"I want you to be that person," she whispered.

Noah wrapped his arms around her and kissed her passionately. Her body perked at his touch, and for the first time since Cooper's death, she felt alive. She gripped his shirt tightly, afraid he'd leave at any second realizing that his feelings were all wrong. But he hugged her tighter, kissing her lips and neck.

He stopped, and she met his dark green eyes with hers. "Are you sure?"

She nodded. "More than anything."

In one swift movement Noah was standing, Sage's legs wrapped around his waist as he carried her to her bedroom.

Cooper watched Noah carry *his* Sage to her bedroom, mouth open. He hadn't been gone long before realizing leaving Sage alone with Noah was a bad idea. He got back just in time to see Sage lower herself over Noah. The thought of it would've made him vomit if he hadn't been a ghost.

He rushed to her door and stopped himself. He heard her say she wanted this. He saw the way she kissed Noah back. Sage's soft moan whispered through the door. She wasn't fighting him off, she was enjoying herself. Maybe

Noah was right all along. Maybe it was time to give Sage the room she needed to move on with her life. The thought made his heart ache. How could she be in there with him?

Cooper headed toward the lake. He needed to clear his head, think of his next move, and there was no way he could concentrate knowing what was going on in that room. He saw his father fly-fishing just down the path and went to him. He was afraid to be alone, afraid his initial thought of barging in on Sage and Noah or causing the entire electrical system to blow would come back.

He wanted to be mad. He wanted to be so angry that he wouldn't think twice about squashing Noah like a roach. But oddly enough, he didn't feel mad or angry, only sad.

She's in there with him. Cooper said to Lucas. *At this moment the love of my life is sleeping with another man. I don't know how I'm supposed to feel about this, Dad. I want to be angry, but all I feel is sadness. She's my girl, always has been, always will be. Sage was fine with being alone until he came into her life. Why did she have to fall for him? Why is he the man that makes her happy?*

I guess I always thought she'd never love anyone but me. Maybe she doesn't love him. I understand women have needs, but she said she wanted him. Maybe I should go into the light and leave her alone. Maybe the carpenter was right all along. What do you think, Dad?

Lucas continued to fish, and Cooper laughed to himself. *Never thought I'd be confiding in you.*

Cooper sat at the water's edge for a long time. Every memory he had of Sage rushed through his head like an old black and white movie. Their love had been epic, but he had been dead over a year. But she still wept for him. She still loved him, regardless of Noah. There was no way he was going to bow out of Sage's life without a fight. They could still be together.

Cooper stood. *I'm not giving up on her. I don't care that she's in there with him. She doesn't know I'm here or she wouldn't be. If Finnley won't tell her I'm here, I'll just have to find a way to show her.*

Chapter 29

Sage studied Noah's face as he slept. He was a picture perfect angel lying in bed next to her. He opened his eyes and smiled. "Good morning."

Sage smiled back. "I believe it's technically afternoon."

Noah caressed her cheek. "Details."

Snuggling in close, she kissed him. "As much as I hate to, I have to get up."

He wrapped her up in a big hug. "No, let's just stay in bed all day."

She kissed him again, a bit longer this time. The temptation to do just as he asked was strong. She pouted her lips. "I really can't, but how about I meet you in this same spot tonight?"

Noah groaned and rolled over, releasing his grip. "I guess, although I'm not sure how I'm supposed to wait that long."

Sage got out of bed and headed toward the shower. "The anticipation will make tonight even better."

Noah jumped up to follow her, a sly smile on his face. "Maybe, but as for now, I think we better conserve water."

Sage hummed a light tune as she entered the kitchen. Her smiled widened as she thought about Noah and their shower tryst. They spent the greater part of the afternoon wrapped in each other's arms, and she couldn't wait to spend the greater part of the evening doing the same thing. But right now there was work to be done.

She slid her iPod into the speaker dock and did a little dance as she made her way to the bar. Pulling out her cookbook, she began to make the menu for the following week. If she hurried, she could still make it to the store.

Lucas sat across from her. "You're glowing. A full house does your soul good."

Sage grinned. "It does indeed."

"And maybe 'other' things have done your soul good, as well?" Lucas raised an eyebrow.

Sage felt a surge of color flow to her cheeks. She searched Lucas's face, trying to figure out exactly how much he knew.

He chuckled and stood. "You should add trout to the menu this week. The fish are biting." He patted her hand. "A happy soul looks great on you. You'll find no judgment here."

"Thanks." Sage exhaled. "You know, for the trout."

Lucas nodded and walked to his room, closing the door gently behind him.

Sage concentrated on the menu while lightly singing with the music.

Cooper stared at the iPod, soon the device started scanning through the music bank. He stopped it when he found what he was looking for. Sage dropped her pencil as the soft tune filled the air.

It was their song, hers and Coopers. The haunting melody brought flashes of their time together as shame filled her heart. She lunged at the device and hit shuffle. Shaking her head, she whispered to herself, "It's just a coincidence. Cooper is not here. He is never coming back. You are allowed to be happy."

Cooper switched the iPod back to their song. Sage stared at the speakers. How? She looked around the room. "Cooper, is that you?"

I'm here baby, he whispered in her ear. *I told you I'm never leaving you again, and I meant it. You don't have to play "house" with the hired help. You can have me. We can be together forever.*

Sage felt a soft breeze against her ear as warm tears ran down her cheeks. "What have I done? Coop, I'm so sorry."

It's okay, baby. I forgive you.

The music shut off. Sage looked up to find Noah holding the iPod in his hand, having unplugged it from the speakers.

"Sage," he said softly, "you've done nothing wrong."

She turned her back to him. He walked around the bar and turned her to face him.

"Talk to me," he pleaded.

She doesn't want to talk to you. You're the cause of all this.

Sage opened her mouth, wanting to explain the situation, but it sounded ludicrous. She could hear the conversation in her mind: Oh, don't mind me. I'm pretty sure I'm being haunted by my dead boyfriend and he just played our song. Now I think we've made a huge mistake, because I'm in love with a ghost. Go ahead and take me to the funny farm. I deserve it.

Her thoughts were interrupted by the doorbell. She grabbed a towel and quickly dried her eyes. "Will you get that?" she asked Noah.

He nodded. Sage looked at herself in the toaster. If anyone asked, she could say she was having an allergy attack. Hopefully, it was just the mailman with a package.

"Hey, stranger, if you can pull yourself away from that toaster for a minute, I need a room."

Sage whirled around to see Richard, bag in hand, grinning from ear to ear.

Noah watched Sage plaster a smile on her face. "Richard, what are you doing here? I thought after our lunch that you'd . . ."

"Never mind our lunch. I should've known better than to ask you what I did." Richard's face flushed with concern. "Are you okay, Sage?"

He looked at Noah. "What happened?"

Nothing really, Richard. She's just realizing there's only one man for her, and it ain't you either.

Sage playfully slapped Richard with the towel. "Nothing happened. You're such a cop. I'm just having an allergy attack. Lots of pollen in the air today. Now what's this you were saying about needing a room?"

Richard raised an eyebrow. "Because I am a cop, I know when people are lying." He glanced at Noah and then back at Sage. "Just know I'm here if you need to talk."

Cooper rolled his eyes. *She doesn't need to talk. She doesn't need either of you. She has me.*

"I appreciate that, Richard." She patted his hand. "Seriously, are you checking in? Or is this you coming to say good-bye?"

"No, I'm not leaving just yet." Richard smiled. "But, if you've got the room, I have a few vacation days I need to use before I lose them. Thought I'd come out here, do some backpacking, fly-fishing, and enjoy some good cooking." He nodded toward the cookbook. "What's on the menu?"

"Well, Lucas just said the trout are biting, so I hope you like grilled trout. It'll take me an hour or so to get your room ready. I have to admit I'm a bit behind after our busy weekend."

Richard hoisted a black backpack onto his shoulder. "No worries. My suitcase is in the car. It'll keep until the room is ready. Until then, I'll just go for a hike and leave you to your work, unless you will let me help."

"Richard, you are now technically on vacation. You are to do no cleaning. Go, and by the time you get back, you'll have a room fit for a king," Sage joked.

"Sounds good," said Richard. He turned toward the door. "Um, Sage . . ."

"Yes."

"No one knows I'm here." Richard ran a hand through his thick hair. "I'd like to keep it that way if you don't mind. Not even if the station calls with an emergency. I'm on vacation."

"My lips are sealed." Sage smiled. "Now go, so I can get some work done."

Lucas walked out of his room as Richard went out the front door. "Another guest?"

Sage nodded. "Looks like Richard will be staying with us for a few days."

"Well, I should do some more fishing then. I better earn my keep, or you'll throw me outside with the dog." The corner of his mouth smirked up.

She grinned. "I am a slave driver."

Sage watched Lucas walk toward the lake, pole in hand, Lexi trailing on his heels. She was glad the dog had taken a liking to the old man. She worried when he went fishing alone.

"We need to talk about what happened earlier." Noah broke her trance. With Richard coming in, she had forgotten he was even in the room.

"There's nothing to talk about." Sage made her way to the laundry room and started gathering cleaning supplies.

Oh, there's a whole mess to talk about. Cooper looked at Noah. *It's time you come clean and tell her you can see me. Tell her I'm here so she won't make the same mistake she just made with you again. You know she senses me around, and that's never gonna change. I will prove to her I'm here.*

Noah ignored Cooper and followed Sage. "When I walked in, you were crying and said you'd made a mistake. Were you talking about what happened this afternoon?"

Sage's shoulders slumped. "I don't know. Maybe we did make a mistake."

Damn right, you did.

"How can you say that?" Noah threw his hands up in the air. "This is not some fling. There's something between us. We both feel it. I love you."

"The only thing I feel right now, is that I've cheated on Cooper," Sage blurted.

Noah bowed his head. "Because that song was playing? Or is there something else?"

Because she's mine, Cooper said, hitting the door frame.

"You don't understand." Sage turned to face Noah. "I feel him around me every day. I don't think he's gone. The feeling is so strong that I talk to him, Noah." She shook her head. "Things like that happen all the time. That song playing wasn't a coincidence. It didn't just play once, it came on, and I changed it. Then it came on again, in the middle of another song. It's like Coop was telling me he's here, and he knows what I did. You probably think I'm crazy."

Noah wrapped his arms around her. "No, you're not crazy. You spent years with Cooper by your side. I can't imagine what you've had to go through since his accident."

"I swear to God if you say a part of him will always be with me . . ." Sage pushed Noah away and picked up her cleaning supplies.

"I wasn't going to say that."

"Just stop." Sage held up her hand. "I can't deal with this now. I have to get Richard's room ready and then start supper."

"Let me help," said Noah, grabbing for the bucket.

"No, I've got this. You've got your own stuff to do." She touched his cheek. "We'll talk about this later, I promise."

Chapter 30

Noah watched Sage walk up the stairs before turning to Cooper and grabbing the collar of his shirt. "Don't you move."

He waited until he heard the door upstairs close. Cooper knocked Noah's hand off his shirt, but to Noah's surprise he didn't vanish.

Noah took a deep breath trying to steady his nerves. "Just what do you think you're doing?"

I could ask you the same thing. Did you think I was just going to sit back while you slept with my girl? Cooper growled. *I warned you there would be consequences.*

"She is not your girl anymore." Noah rubbed his jaw. "You're only hurting her by pulling crap like that stunt with the song. Don't you see that? For the love of God, let her move on. You can't love her like she needs to be loved, not anymore."

That's what you want me to think. Cooper shook his head in disgust. *I can't believe she'd settle for a piece of crap like you. You're a parasite, a bottom feeder. I will always be here for her, and you can't do anything about it. I'm growing stronger every day, and soon I'll make her see me. She'll know for certain that I never left her. You only want me to go into the light because you know that's true. You know she won't be able to ignore what's happening around her.*

Noah could feel the heat rising through his chest. "All that talk, and you still missed the point. We both want her to be happy. And from what I can tell, she'll be far happier with me than she ever was with you. You're only a pain in the neck to her, probably always were. You're selfish, Cooper. She deserves better! If you truly love her, you'll let her move on with me."

Cooper ran toward Noah, fist raised. Noah laughed. "What are you going to do, Cooper? Hit me? Don't forget I can hit back."

Even though he saw it coming, the punch knocked the air out of Noah. He was sure Cooper didn't have the energy to really hurt him, but he was wrong. "You know what, I'll take that punch. I slept with the woman you love. I get that. But that's the only one you get."

Cooper smacked Noah squarely in the jaw, causing his teeth to rattle. Noah stared Cooper down. "That's it. I didn't want it to come to this, but I'm throwing your ass into the light. This has gone on long enough. If you won't go on your own, I'll force you to."

The light appeared in front of the pantry door.

I'm not going anywhere.

Cooper took another swing at Noah, but this time Noah was ready and ducked, coming up with a shot to Cooper's stomach.

Pain ripped through Cooper's belly causing him to take a few steps back, a look of surprise on his face.

"What?" said Noah, shrugging his shoulders. "You didn't think I would hit you back? Guess again."

The two men lunged at each other and locked arms, jerking each other around the kitchen like rag dolls as Cooper fought to stay out of the light. Noah was finally able to get Cooper into a headlock, but Cooper disappeared. He reappeared behind Noah and ran full speed into him, knocking him into the couch.

Noah rolled over and kicked Cooper off him, causing him to fly into the fireplace. Candles fell to the floor, along with the wicker wreath that hung over the mantle. Noah stood up and brushed himself off. "Are we finished? Can we stop playing these childish games? Go into the light."

Never!

Cooper ran at Noah once again, slamming him into the kitchen bar, causing the vase of flowers Richard had brought Sage to shatter all over the floor.

"Damn it, Cooper," said Noah.

"What is going on down here?"

Noah froze, there was no way Sage had just walked into the room while he was fighting with Cooper. But there she was standing on the stairs, brandishing a broom like a baseball bat. She looked around the room and then raised an eyebrow.

"I asked you a question, Noah." Sage put the broom down and folded her arms. "It sounded like you were being attacked. I swear if you and Richard have been fighting . . . Tell me, Noah, what's going on?"

Cooper laughed. *Go ahead tell her the truth. See how she reacts when you tell her you could see and hear me the whole time. She'll never want to see you again.*

"Deputy Park has nothing to do with this." Noah cleared his throat. "I never meant to hurt you. Everything I did was for you. I hope you can understand that."

"Right now all I understand is I have a messed up living room and kitchen, and you haven't answered my question."

Totally his fault, said Cooper pointing at Noah. *I told him not to push me, and you know how I get. Besides as soon as you find out he can see me, it won't matter whose fault it is.*

"I'm going to, I promise. Before I do I have to ask you to keep an open mind and hear me out completely."

The color drained from Sage's face as she slowly nodded. "I'll try."

"Okay," Noah ran both hands through his hair. "But you should probably sit down."

Sage sat on the stairs as Noah cleared his throat again and began pacing. "I really don't know how to say this so that it'll make any sense, so let me start here. I meant it when I told you I love you, and I'm not going anywhere. I've always been here for you and will continue to be, no matter how you take this news."

Sure, try and butter her up first. Cooper leaned close to Sage's ear. *Sweetheart, he's using me to get to you. I'm the only one who could ever love you the right way.*

"Shut up!" yelled Noah.

Sage flinched. "You're starting to scare me, Noah. Do I need to call an ambulance? Are you having a breakdown? I'm sure I can find Richard to help."

Noah shook his head, closed his eyes, and took in a deep breath. "As you know, I was hesitant to go into a partnership with you here at Winter Song. But what you don't know is the reason."

"I don't see what that has to do with the mess I see here," said Sage. "Listen, whatever it is we'll get you help.

I'll say he needs it, snorted Cooper.

"Did I do this? With the whole iPod/Cooper thing and what we did this afternoon?" Sage asked in a soft whisper.

That would be an understatement.

"It had nothing to do with you or what happened this afternoon." Noah kneeled in front of Sage. His heart ached as he thought of the last time he knelt in front of her and the glorious afternoon it had led to. "It had to do with Cooper."

"Cooper?" Sage raised an eyebrow. "I wasn't aware that you knew him."

"I didn't. Well, I heard about him and the accident, but no, I didn't know Cooper when he was alive."

"You really aren't making sense, Noah. Do you need a glass of water or something? Did you bump your head?" Sage started to get up, but Noah stopped her.

"I've gotten to know Cooper since I've been here. Since living at Winter Song. He's still here . . . with you."

"Okay," Sage said, slowly. "I didn't realize I talked that much about him, but I guess I can see how you got to know him through Lucas and me. But I still don't get what's going on and why you broke the vase. And I swear I heard you say Cooper's name."

Noah studied her face, waiting for everything he had told her to sink in. He could see her going over the conversation in her mind, putting the puzzle pieces together.

Suddenly, her eyes widened. "Noah, are you trying to tell me that you see ghosts?"

"No, Sage, it's more than that. I see Cooper."

Chapter 31

"I've always been able to see spirits . . . ," said Noah, pausing to judge Sage's reaction. ". . . ever since I was a little boy, so, yes, I can see and hear Cooper."

Sage started laughing. Noah rubbed his jaw.

"So Cooper's here?" Sage gasped through a snort laugh. "And he's been here since he died? Doing what? Following me around like a puppy dog? And he's been here the whole time you've been here? He's been talking to you since you've started working here, and you've never said one word about it to me? Let me guess, he's in the room right now."

I'm right here, baby, said Cooper, standing behind Sage. *We'll get this all worked out so we can be together again.*

Noah looked at Cooper and rolled his eyes.

"Yes, that's all true," Noah mumbled, "he's been trying to get me to talk for him from day one, but I said no."

"And how do I know this isn't just a big scheme?" asked Sage.

Noah leaned down in front of Sage. "I know I've been here for months and never said anything, but I swear I have never lied to you, and I would never try to scheme or play you."

What? You've been lying all along! Just can't help yourself can ya, Finnley?

"And I never will lie to you," Noah continued ignoring Cooper. "You never asked me if I could talk to Cooper; therefore, I never lied to you about whether I could or not."

"Like that would ever come up in conversation?" mocked Sage. "Oh, hey, guy I just met, could you come help me on my place, and by any chance, can you see dead people? I'd love to talk to my ex-boyfriend." Sage started laughing again. "Is this a joke?"

Tell her the song on the radio is ours because we shared our first kiss while it played. We were sitting in her mother's beat up yellow station wagon we nicknamed The Wiz after a junior high football game.

"It's no joke," said Noah. "Cooper says you two had your first kiss in a station wagon named The Wiz after a football game, and that's how you got your song."

Sage's hand flew up to her mouth as tears fell on her cheeks. She studied his face, searching for an impossible answer. "How could you know that? You really can see him? Why didn't you tell me? You've been here for months. After this afternoon, you didn't think Cooper being here was information I needed to know?"

"That's not the sort of thing I do. I don't talk for the dead," said Noah. "I think it's better for spirits to move into the light and let their loved ones have some peace. It really is the best for everyone involved."

Sage's eyes narrowed. "*You* think? How would *you* even know? Who are you to make that kind of decision?"

Noah leaned in, searching Sage's face for understanding. "From my experience these 'good-bye' messages cause more harm than good. People hang onto the thought that their loved one is near. They don't say good-bye because they don't have to. How is anyone supposed to move on and gain closure if they're constantly talking to a ghost? It drives people mad. It did my Mom."

"Your mom?" Sage's eyes softened.

Noah paused, swallowing the lump that grew in his throat. "When my dad died, I could still see him. I was only seven, so I told my mom. I just figured she could see him too."

Noah looked up, willing gravity to force the tears to remain in place. "For the next ten years, I watched her live in a fantasy world with me relaying message after message from my father. She was so lonely, but wouldn't dare be with someone else because my dad was always around."

He wiped his cheeks, the tears having escaped. "I couldn't go anywhere because my mom constantly needed me to be around to relay messages. She started using drugs, trying to see him for herself."

"One day she slit her wrists, and Becca found her." Noah swallowed hard. "All of us knew it couldn't go on. So we put Mom in rehab. Dad agreed to go into the light, and I agreed to leave home. Mom died in that place. Her heart just gave out one day."

Noah took a deep breath. "The doctors said it was due to the drug use, but she came to me after she died and told me it was due to a broken heart. She couldn't live without my dad, so she wanted to die so she could be with him again.

"She was so mad at herself for stealing my childhood." Noah folded his arms. "She made me promise I would never talk to another ghost. I swore to her, right then and there, I would never do that to another person. I would never give someone false hope that they could once again be with the person they loved. I've managed to avoid most ghosts until now."

He looked at Sage, tears flooding her face. "So when Cooper asked me to relay messages to you, I couldn't. Don't you see? I couldn't do to you what I did to my mother all those years ago. I've been trying to convince him to go into the light, so you'll both have peace. And in the meantime, I fell in love with you, so there was a part of me that didn't want you to know he was still here. This afternoon I felt we were finally coming to a place that would make us both happy, regardless of Cooper."

Sage gasped. "Did he see what happened this afternoon? Does he know?"

It's alright, Sage. I forgive you. It's all Finnley's fault.

Noah nodded. "He didn't see it, but he knows. That's why he played that song on your iPod. He wanted you to know that he knew. He wanted you to feel guilty so you'd tell me to leave, since I won't relay his messages anyway."

"Where is he?" Sage asked, looking around the room.

"This is a bad idea," Noah started.

"Just tell me where he is!" she yelled, standing.

Noah sighed. "He's standing right behind you."

Cooper touched Sage's hair. *I'm right here, baby. I'll always be right here. I'm never going to leave you again. I promise.*

Sage felt her hair move. "Was that him? Behind me?"

Noah nodded.

"I bet he's done that a million times since he died. How long as he been here?"

I never left you, baby. I've been here the whole time. I promised I'd never leave you, and I haven't. Cooper caressed her hair again.

"He says he's never left you," Noah relayed.

Her brows furrowed, right before she turned around and swung at the air, her fist going right through Cooper's face.

What the . . .? Cooper staggered back even though the blow went through him.

"How dare you say you've been here the entire time. You left me, remember? You think you can come back here after dying and make me feel bad for moving on?" Sage yelled into the air. "I told you not to get on that stupid boat, but you didn't listen to me. You didn't care how I felt about it. Then you died, and now you want me to put my life on hold until I die. You are a selfish coward, Cooper Davis."

Noah came up behind her and placed his hands on her shoulders. "It's okay, Sage. We can work this out. Cooper can still go into the light. Everything's going to be okay."

"Get your hands off me." She shrugged him away, turned, and slapped him. "You should've told me. You're no better than he is. You've been lying to me this whole time, saying you talk to yourself. I can't believe I fell for that crap. You two have been talking about me since you got here. Is this your big plan? Find out all the goods on me to get me into bed."

Sage headed toward the door.

"Sage, wait! It's not like that." Noah scrambled after her. "Let's talk about this, the three of us. Let's just get it settled so we can all move on."

Sage jerked the door open. "Stay away from me, both of you."

She slammed the door and headed toward the forest.

Good job, Finnley. Cooper snorted. *Now she's pissed at both of us. You should've just come clean from the start.*

"Don't act like you're innocent in all this." Noah rubbed his jaw, which still burned from Sage's slap.

At least yours was open fisted, remarked Cooper. *Had I been alive, she would've knocked me out.* He looked out the window. *I'm going after her. I don't like the idea of her being out there alone in her state of mind.*

"Don't," said Noah. "The least we can do is respect her privacy right now. She needs to think, and we need to give her the space to do so."

She'll never know I'm there, Cooper retorted.

"I know and I'll tell her." Noah shook his head. "I'm not lying to her again."

Chapter 32

Sage ran once she hit the path. She knew running was silly. Noah didn't dare follow her, and even if Cooper did, she'd never know, not to mention she couldn't outrun a ghost. But it felt good to pound down the path with each step. Her sides began to ache. As she felt her chest tighten she decided she'd better walk. Besides, running up on a bear would make her day even worse.

She sat on a rock to catch her breath. She didn't know who she was madder at -- Coop for sticking around, not going into the light, and making her feel badly for moving on? Or Noah for lying to her and not passing on Coop's message? She understood why Noah was hesitant. The thought of what Noah went through with his mother made Sage's stomach hurt. Besides would Coop have gone into the light after Noah relayed his message? Probably not. Coop had always been territorial, especially when it came to her.

She thought about the time when she worked the night shift at the hotel with her co-worker, Gary. Sage hadn't realized how much she talked about Gary to Cooper. Truth was Gary was a fun guy to work with and a natural comedian. He made the night shift fly by, and even though she could handle herself, she liked that there was a man behind the desk with her.

What Sage had failed to mention to Cooper was that she had also met Gary's lovely wife on a number of occasions. So it came as some surprise to Cooper to find Gary flirting with a spunky red-head when he dropped by the hotel.

"Quite the ladies man aren't you?" Cooper confronted a stunned Gary.

"He better not be," laughed the red-head.

"You can do better, lady," said Cooper. "In fact, I'm here to tell him he doesn't have a chance with Sage. She's taken. Got that, pal?"

"Cooper Davis, how dare you come into my place of work and start trouble," Sage scolded, coming around the corner.

"I'm glad you're here, Sage," said Cooper, a smug smile across his face. "This Gary you talk about all the time is here flirting with this lady."

"Well, I would hope so, Coop," said Sage. "She's his wife. She comes in every evening and brings Gary dinner."

Gary held up a plate covered in aluminum foil confirming what Sage had said.

Sage sighed. "Gary is my friend only. I spend almost every night working with him. Of course I'm gonna talk about him. By the time I get home, you're off to work and vice versa. He's really the only person I talk to other than the guests. Now, get over yourself."

Sage didn't talk to Cooper for a whole week after he embarrassed her like that with his petty jealousy. That was the only time she gave serious thought to if she wanted to be in a relationship with someone with territorial tendencies. But she gave him credit for apologizing to both Gary and his wife, plus herself. She told him that kind of thing wouldn't fly with her, and he never did anything like that again. Until Noah.

Sage's thoughts turned to Noah. She couldn't get over how he kept her from Coop. Then she thought about Noah's mom and how hard that had to be on him. She couldn't imagine the guilt he must feel. The guilt she felt for having feelings for another man was no match for the death of a mother. Sage stood and started walking again, stepping off the trail in case Noah got a wild hair to follow her. She craved the isolation of the deep, dark forest. She needed to think.

Once again, her thoughts turned to Coop. He had no right to play that song after finding out about her and Noah. The minute he left for that stupid ship he gave up all rights to the sympathy card. She begged him not to go, her gut telling her it would end badly.

Of course, she never thought he would die. More than likely he'd get arrested after punching a captain or crew member. She imagined him in the cold Bering Sea, fighting for every last breath. He must've been thinking about her as he waited to die. How else would he have gotten back to her?

Lost in thought, she didn't realize she had walked up on Richard until it was too late. There he stood, shovel in hand, standing over a deep hole.

"Richard, you startled me." She looked at the shovel in his hand. "You would not believe the day I've had."

Richard shook his head. "You shouldn't be here."

"What do you mean?" She placed her hands on her hips, studying the hole. "What are you doing? You know I don't allow traps or hunting here."

"Just turn around, Sage, and forget you saw anything," said Richard. "You didn't want any part of my big plan, so now you need to leave."

Sage glanced down at the unzipped black backpack Richard took on the trail with him. Bundles of hundred dollar bills spilled out onto the forest floor.

"I'm not going anywhere." Sage planted her feet. "Where did you get that money? Why are you burying it out here?"

"Seriously, Sage, just go. I'll grab my stuff, get in my car, and leave. We'll pretend you didn't see anything." Richard started filling in the hole.

"I don't understand, Richard." Sage shook her head. "What are you doing with all that cash? I swear every man in my life has gone crazy today."

"You needn't worry about me. You should really worry about yourself. I never wanted you to see any of this part. I just wanted you to come with me after the dirty work was taken care of." Richard leaned on the shovel. He let out a low laugh before pulling a gun out of his back pocket and pointing it at her. "Now you've left me no choice. Why couldn't you just turn around?"

Sage eyes sharpened with understanding as she raised her hands slowly and started to back up. "You're right. This is none of my business. Just wanted to know if you'd prefer grilled squash or corn on the cob with the trout. I'll probably just go with corn on the cob. They had some good looking cobs at the Farmer's Market last week. I was going to swing by there anyway."

She turned back toward the trail. "I'll see you at dinner."

"Sage, stop," Richard bellowed, cocking the gun. Sage paused. "I won't let anyone ruin this for me. I'll shoot you if I have to. Don't make me go there."

"Put the gun down, Richard," Sage said slowly as she turned to face him. "You're scaring me. You can do whatever you want out here."

"Don't you see?" Richard waved the gun around his supplies. "You've seen too much. I can't let you go now."

"I haven't seen anything," Sage let out a nervous giggle. "People dig holes in the ground for all sorts of reasons." She smiled weakly. "I'm not here to judge. I'm just going to go home and take a hot bath. By the time I'm out, you'll be gone. No harm, no foul."

"Do you think I'm stupid?" Richard narrowed his eyes. "I know you've seen the cash. You're a smart girl. You know honest people don't bury their cash in the woods. The minute you get back to Winter Song, you'll call the police. Now be a good girl and come here."

Sage froze for an instant before dodging to her left and running. She heard Richard curse behind her as tree branches snapped. She chastised herself for stepping off the trail, bushwhacking at a steady run was near impossible. She tripped on a root, causing her to fall to the ground, ripping her jeans.

She jumped up but could feel Richard even closer. Continuing to zig zag she prayed Noah was looking for her. Coop would be here. There's no way Cooper would leave her alone. He would tell Noah she was in trouble. Finally, she spotted the trail ahead of her. Her foot touched the smooth ground just as Richard's firm hand yanked her around to face him.

"No!" Sage's scream echoed throughout the valley.

Chapter 33

Lucas let the fly dance on the slow rapids before pulling on the line. A small trout nibbled at it, but Lucas jerked the fly away. No need to put the little guy through a lip piercing when he was after the big fellows. He turned back toward Lexi who sat on the bank gazing down the trail.

"Should not have told Sage the fish were biting. I went and made the lake gods mad by bragging." Lucas told the dog. "Probably won't catch another trout all season."

Lexi's ears perked up, and she stood, legs tensed.

"What is it, girl?" Lucas asked, reeling in his line. "What's wrong?"

Before Lucas could gather his line in, Lexi took off running. He tried to follow, only to lose his balance on the river rocks and splash into the water. All he could do was watch Lexi's tail as she barreled down the trail, leaving him in her dust.

Lucas picked himself up out of the water and slowly trudged toward the shore. "Stupid dog, probably after a mangy ol' rabbit." Shaking the excess water off, he made his way to the house. He could see Noah standing on the porch, watching the trail.

"A little chilly for a swim, isn't it?" asked Noah, grabbing the blanket off the porch swing and handing it to Lucas.

"Lexi took off like the devil himself was after her. I tried to follow." Lucas smiled. "I guess I'm not as limber as the dog."

Noah's eyes narrowed in thought.

"What's going on?" Lucas asked.

Noah sighed. "You're going to find out eventually, so I'll just tell you now. Sage found out I can see and speak to your son. She ran off into the woods about half an hour ago. She's pretty mad at me. I'm just giving her some space, waiting for her to come back so we can work everything out."

Lucas looked at the ground, mumbling something to himself. His head shot up as gestured toward the path. "Go, now!"

"She wants to be left alone." Noah held up his hands. "I've got to respect that and wait for her here."

"No," Lucas gasped, "Remember when Sage ran into the bear? Lexi acted the same way that day. I think Sage is in trouble. That's why Lexi took off. I'll wait here in case Sage comes back." He opened the back door and looked at Noah. "Go, you fool!"

"Don't make this harder than it has to be," Richard said, squeezing Sage's arm, trying to drag her off the path.

Sage tried to shrug him off, but his grip held. "Let me go, Richard. This won't end well for you. Just come back to

Winter Song, and we'll work everything out. It doesn't have to be this way."

"I can't let you go. But if you'll stop fighting me for one minute, I can explain." Richard loosened his grip a bit. "This was the perfect plan, and you had to go muck it all up. You should've just agreed to go with me. We've been friends for a long time. Will you give me a chance?"

Sage gave him a quick nod.

"It's like I was telling you at lunch. I'm so sick of this town. Everyone has something to complain about and for some reason, I'm the local go-to guy for the gripe fests. Most of the time it has nothing to do with breaking the law. It's just people complaining about their neighbor's lawn ornaments or roosters crowing at 5:00 a.m., really petty stuff. I just couldn't take it anymore."

Richard took a deep breath, then continued. "So I robbed the bank down at Rock Creek. My original plan was for us to travel the world, to see everything you've ever wanted to see. We'd stay in grand hotels and villas and be treated like royalty. But since you wouldn't come with me, I decided I would just retire and stay out here with you to help with Winter Song. I was just going to bring out the money a little at a time, make it look like savings. That way we could travel a bit during the off season. See the world."

"How in the world did you think you were going to get away with this?" asked Sage.

"Rock Creek Bank doesn't have any surveillance or security, so I got away scot-free. Being a cop, I could easily find out when their next armored truck stop was and hit the bank an hour or so before they collected the money. I came out here this weekend to convince you to fire Noah Finnley and let me take his place. I was so hurt that you wouldn't come with me. But after thinking about it, I realized you were right, and I want to make your dream of Winter Song come true. Your dream is my dream. With my help and the money from the bank, we can make this the best bed and breakfast in the state, and we'll be able to do it together. I know we can make each other happy." He eyed Sage. "So what do you think, Sage?"

"What do I think about what?" Sage raised an eyebrow. "That you robbed a bank or that you expected just to waltz out here, have me fire Noah, and then use me to launder your loot? Did you think I was too stupid to realize you had all this money all of a sudden? Your plan not only jeopardizes Winter Song, it puts my life in danger. I don't want to spend the rest of my life in prison for helping out a bank robber. You don't really care about me and my dreams at all. It's all about what you want."

"It's not like that." Richard once again tightened his grip. "I love you, Sage. I want to share this dream with you. I know you feel it, too. I know you want to be more than friends."

Sage shook her head. "I'm sorry, Richard. That's not how I feel."

"You're lying to me because you're scared after having your heart broken by Cooper," said Richard. "I would never do anything to hurt you. I've loved you since the moment I met you. Cooper just got to you first. I waited for the day the two of you would break up, but you never did. He was such a screw up, and you just kept giving him chance after chance. Till he left town."

Richard looked at his feet before returning his stare to Sage. "I never wanted him to die, but I prayed he'd never come back. I hoped he'd find some Alaskan woman to love and leave you. Then I'd be there to pick up the pieces. And I have been, haven't I, Sage? I've always been there for you. I love you, and I know you love me too. Just say the words and make all this worth it."

Sage ripped her arm out of Richard's gasp. "Richard, I don't love you."

"You're just afraid to say it because you've never said it to anyone but Cooper," explained Richard.

Sage shook her head. "No, Richard, that isn't it. I love Noah."

The words escaped her mouth before she could take them back. She watched his face turn an awful shade of red as he raised the gun again.

"You love the handyman? How could you love him? You barely know him. You've known me since we were children." Richard slowly shook his head. "He can't have you. I've waited too long for you to be free of Cooper. I will not just have you fall into the arms of another man. No one else can have you!"

Without thinking, Sage kicked Richard as hard as she could between the legs. He buckled over in pain, dropping the gun. She took off running down the path.

She ran faster than she thought possible but could still feel Richard on her heels even after the kick to the groin. If she could make it a few more feet, she could dive back into the brush and lose Richard for good. She just needed a little time to get away. A smile crossed her face as she saw Lexi barreling towards her.

Sage rolled to the ground as Lexi leaped over her, tearing into Richard.

"Get him, girl!" Sage yelled as she watched in horror. She knew she should run, but her faith was in Lexi. She would save her.

Lexi snarled and snapped at Richard, causing him to fall to the ground. He kicked at the dog, but she remained vigilant, chomping at his arms to get to his face. A sharp yelp echoed through the air as the gun went off. Lexi went limp.

Chapter 34

Noah stopped dead in his tracks after hearing the gun fire. Cooper appeared by his side.

Was that what I think it was? Cooper asked. *Tell me that was not a gun shot.*

"It was definitely a gun shot," said Noah. "Maybe it was a hunter."

Cooper shook his head. *No, Sage wouldn't allow any hunting, and it's off season. I'm not waiting for you. I'm going to find her.*

"I don't expect you to wait. Just make sure she's okay," Noah said gravely.

Cooper disappeared, and Noah veered off the trail. The trail was easier, but it also made him a sitting duck for anyone looking for target practice. He picked his way carefully through the brush, searching for clues, hoping he wouldn't be watching Sage go into the light with Cooper.

A patch of white caught his eye on the path. A lump grew in his throat as he recalled the white shirt Sage had been wearing when she took off down the path.

"Please, God, don't let it be her," he whispered.

He cautiously approached, and released a breath he hadn't been aware he was holding when he realized it was Lexi. He looked both ways, leery of being out in the open. He watched for a sign that the dog was still alive. He really needed to be looking for Sage, but she'd never forgive him if he didn't help Lexi. The dog whimpered once. Noah found himself smiling, knowing she was still alive. He slowly walked to her. Putting his hand by her nose first, he gently rubbed her head.

"It'll be okay," he said softly.

She was breathing hard, but she was still breathing. A bullet hole oozed blood just under her front shoulder.

"You're a good girl," he cooed to the dog. "I don't want to leave you, but I *must* help Sage. Just lie still. Someone will be here shortly to get you."

As if summoned, Lucas appeared out of the brush and bent close to the dog. Lexi wagged her tail a little at the sight of the old man.

"I'm not even going to ask you how you got here so quickly," Noah said. "I'm just glad you're here."

"Never underestimate the gods of the wind or the will of an old man." Noah helped Lucas pick up Lexi and he started back toward Winter Song. "Go! Sage is still out there. You must find her. My son cannot do it alone."

"Stupid dog. Where the hell did she even come from?" Richard dragged Sage back toward the clearing where the money still laid on the ground. He looked at the bite wound on his arm. "I hope that mutt of yours has been vaccinated."

Richard groaned and slid the gun into the back of his jeans. "There's no way your boyfriend didn't hear that shot back at the house. I'm sure he's on the path right now looking for his lover. I can't believe you think you're in love with him. In time you'll see. It's me you want."

Cooper appeared at Sage's side. *Thank God I found you. Are you okay? Have you been shot?*

He looked her over, sighing with relief when he found no bullet hole or blood.

"I'll never want you. You're a monster." Tears streamed down Sage's face as she chastised herself for not running while Lexi had Richard distracted. "I can't believe you shot Lexi," she screamed at Richard. "She was just protecting me."

"Protecting you from what? Me? That dog is rabid. I did you a favor," sneered Richard. "I should've shot her the first day I found out about her."

You son of a bitch, you shot my dog? Cooper advanced on Richard and swung wildly, his fists finding nothing but air. His energy was still spent from the fight with Noah. *Damn it!*

"You're acting like I'm the bad guy here," said Richard matter-of-factly.

"You are the one with the gun," Sage retorted, sarcastically.

Richard, what is going on here? Why did you shoot Lexi? Cooper eyed the money bag. *I'm your friend. What's with the gun? You're acting like a crazy man.*

Swooping up the bag of money, Richard dug deep inside the bag pulling out a stretch of rope. "We can't stay here now. We have to move."

"Where are we going? Just let me go. I'll only slow you down." Sage once again tried to shrug off Richard's firm grasp as he tied her hands together. "Ouch, Richard. Stop. You're hurting me."

What are you doing, you S.O. B.? Let her go! Cooper went in for a tackle this time, trying to knock Richard to the ground as he had done to Noah early. Again he ran right through him and Sage.

Cooper looked to the sky. *Why won't you help me? I promise, God, I'll go into the light if you'll just let Sage be okay. Help me help her, please.*

Richard glared at Sage, pulling her close before attaching the other end of rope to his belt. "Like that little kick to the jewels didn't hurt me? You're the one who broke my heart." He pulled her face close to his, causing her to flinch. "Besides, if I let you go and then you run, I'll have to shoot you. And I'd rather not do that. This day's been bad enough already. I'd hate to kill the woman I love as well. So now you're coming with me. You're my ticket to Canada."

Woman you love? What in the world is going on?

Sage gasped. "Canada? You've robbed a bank, Richard. They're not just going to invite you in."

Robbed a bank? Richard? The whole world has gone insane.

"And just how do you suppose we get there? It's a two-day drive," continued Sage. "Just let me go. I'll tell Noah you've left, and you can go anywhere you want. You don't need me. I'll only slow you down."

"Pretty soon, your boyfriend will have this place crawling with cops. While they're searching the woods, we'll backtrack and get a car," explained Richard. "If they corner me or get too close, I'll have you to keep them at bay. They aren't going to do anything to me if I've got you."

Cooper got as close as he could to Sage. *I'm here, baby. You're going to be okay. I'll let Noah know the plan. This jerk will not get away with this. I'll be right back, baby. You're not alone. I love you.*

Cooper took one last look at Sage before concentrating on Noah's location. He was getting pretty good at appearing by people's sides when he concentrated. Although he'd give anything to exchange that little superpower for one that allowed him to knock Richard Park into the ground.

Noah was picking his way through the brush, looking for clues when Cooper appeared.

"Did you find her?" he asked. "Is she okay?"

Yeah, she's scared, but okay. Richard has taken her hostage. He's the one who shot Lexi. They're north of here about a mile. He's staying off the main path. He's waiting for the cops to swarm the woods so he can backtrack to Winter Song and steal a car. He's using Sage as leverage. We have to stop him!

"Deputy Park?" Noah asked. "What the hell is he doing?"

Sage said something about him robbing a bank, and he has a backpack full of cash so it makes sense. Cooper clenched his fist. *I tried to help her, but I can't touch the bastard. I spent all my energy fighting you earlier.*

"Is he leaving Sage in the woods somewhere, then going for the car?" asked Noah. "If so, we can just wait until he leaves, then you can lead me to her."

Cooper shook his head. *No, he's taking her to Canada. Says she's his ticket in. He says he's in love with her, and he knows about you. He called you her "little boyfriend." I don't think he's your biggest fan right now. In fact, I'm pretty sure he'll shoot you on sight.*

"Go back to her," said Noah. "He'll have to stop soon. It's getting dark. I'll continue to head in that direction. There's no way I'm going back to Winter Song with Sage out here. Do whatever you can to stall him. I'll be there as soon as I can. It's up to you now."

Chapter 35

"We'll stop here." Richard shoved Sage to the ground and tied her to a tree. It'll be dark soon, and they won't attempt a search party until daybreak anyway."

"Do you really think you're going to get away with this?" she asked. "By now they know it's you. You're the only other one on the property. Noah would've told the police that by now."

"For all they know, you and I are off in the woods having some kind of tryst, and your little boyfriend is just jealous. The local cops would never believe I was out here doing something shady anyway," Richard said as he began making a fire, knowing the brush was too thick to be seen from the trail. "I've never so much as jaywalked. They're not going to believe I shot a dog without good reason. They probably won't even come out here. Technically, you won't be a missing person until twenty-four hours have gone by. By then we'll be long gone."

"What are you doing? I thought we were going back to Winter Song." Sage pulled on the ropes, trying to loosen the grip. "You need a car, remember? We can't walk to Canada."

"I changed my mind. It'll be hours before they get enough manpower up here to search these woods. One thing about living in the sticks, there isn't much law to get in your way." Richard produced a wicked smile. "Another good thing about living in the sticks is that everyone is such a dumbass it'll take them hours to realize I'm actually the one who pulled everything off. For all they know, we're both in trouble. They won't start a search until morning, too dangerous not knowing how many perps are out here with guns. Going back to Winter Song now would be like walking into their hands. We'll wait here until after midnight. Then we'll sneak back, and you'll write a pretty little note explaining that the bed and breakfast scene isn't for you, and you've asked me to take you away from it all."

"Noah will never believe that, and if you really think he's not out here trying to find me, you're delusional." Sage's face softened. "Just let me go, Richard. I'm so turned around right now it'll take me all night to find my way back, and even then I won't be able to tell them where you are."

"You always pick the wrong guys." Richard shook his head as the fire flared up. "And I bet you know exactly where we are, but it'll take your new lover boy hours to find us." He patted his gun. "And there's a huge part of me that hopes he does."

"Leave Noah out of this. He's done nothing to you." Sage bowed her head.

"I don't know how you do it, Sage," continued Richard. "You always seem to find the worst men. First, it was Cooper. What a good-for-nothing piece of garbage. The man couldn't keep a job if his life depended on it. If he were still alive, you guys would still be living in that one bedroom shack you called a cabin. It was better that he died. At least that way you could finally afford Winter Song."

"Shut up." More tears burned in Sage's eyes. "How can you say those things? He was your friend."

"Friend?" Richard let out a snort laugh. "He was a thorn in the side of our lives. You know I'm telling the truth, Sage. You worked your butt off trying to save money, and every time someone looked at him wrong, he quit, causing you to dip into your savings to pay the bills. Now there's the carpenter, who as far as I can tell, is just another mooch taking a ride on the ol' Sage train. For the love of God, he was getting kicked out of his apartment for failure to pay rent, and you just up and hired him. Not only did you hire him, but you let him move in."

Richard knelt to meet Sage's eyes. "And here I've been, in love with you for all these years. I remained your friend because that's all you'd let me be, and I've been the best kind of friend. I've gotten Cooper out of trouble more times than I can count. I've done everything in my power to see to your happiness. Then he died, and I thought, it's my turn. Finally, Sage will see me as more than a friend." Richard licked his lips. "But no, you had to go and fall for the stupid carpenter!"

"You're right," whispered Sage.

"What?" Richard raised an eyebrow.

"I said, you're right," Sage continued. "You've always been here for me. Every time I've asked for your help, you've given it without question. Now let me be the same kind of friend to you. Just let me go, and I'll tell Noah and Lucas that everything is okay. I'll tell them that Lexi was shot by a poacher, and you and I were trying to track him down. Then you can take your money and leave. No one will even know you've been here. You can go live the life you've always wanted."

"The life I've always wanted is with you." His eyes full of hope. "If I do all these things you've just asked of me, is there a chance for us?"

Sage looked into Richard's eyes. She wanted to lie. She wanted to tell him that she loved him and that she would go with him, anything to get back to Noah and Winter Song. But the words wouldn't form. She couldn't betray her feelings for Noah even if it meant saving her own life. She closed her eyes.

"I didn't think so," Richard sneered.

He got up and kicked dirt at Sage, causing her to cry out.

"I could never love you! You're a fraction of the men Coop and Noah are," she spat.

Richard knelt down again. "Don't you mean were? Cooper's dead, and soon Noah will join him. Poor, poor Sage. She can't ever get a break. All her lovers die."

"And what about me?" Sage asked. "Are you going to kill me or just keep me captive with the delusion that one day I'll love you back? That will never happen."

"Is that right?" he pressed the gun barrel into her forehead. "I guess I could just kill you now."

Sage closed her eyes tight and waited for the pain of the shot. But Richard pulled the gun away.

"No, Sage, I'm not going to kill you. No, I'm going to do something much worse. When we get back to Winter

Song, I'm gonna kill that old man you've taken in. And then I'm gonna take great pleasure in killing your new boy toy."

He flicked her cheek with the gun. "But you, dear Sage, will live. You will live with the knowledge that your selfishness caused them all to die. And after I've killed everyone in your life at Winter Song, I know you well enough to know you won't be able to stay there. There will be too many memories, and you will want to sell the place, meaning I will have killed your dream as well. And honestly, I doubt you could sell it. A double murder has a way of turning buyers off. So you'll have to stay here and live every day with the guilt."

"No, Richard, you can't," cried Sage. "I'll go with you. Just leave them alone."

"It's too late for that. You've made your bed."

Its okay, honey. Cooper touched her hair, and Sage's eyes lit up. *That's right I'm here. You know I'm here. Noah is on his way.*

"Besides, we could have some serious fun camping out under the stars. With no one around to watch but the owls and 'coons." Richard winked at Sage as he stuck the gun into his waistband. "If I'm going to hell anyway, I might as well make the most of the trip."

Cooper saw goose bumps take over Sage's arms. *You stay away from her, you animal. I'll kill you if you touch her!*

"What do you say, Sage? How 'bout a little roll in the trees?" Richard sat on Sage's thighs and started kissing her neck. She tried to back away, but Richard's knots were too tight. She tried to knee him off, but it wasn't working.

"Please, Richard, don't do this," Sage begged.

"Just close your eyes and enjoy it," said Richard.

Cooper looked around, desperate to get Richard off Sage. He ran to the far side of the campsite and focused on smashing a stick. The snap caused Richard to jump up and grab his gun, slowly making his way to Cooper.

"Is that your lover boy?" Richard called out. "Come on out, Noah. We need to talk."

Richard waited, but when no one came, he turned his attention back to Sage. "Now where were we?"

Cooper was about to rush Richard again when a flash of color behind Sage caught his eye. It was Noah. Cooper snapped another tree further in the brush in the opposite direction, causing Richard to explore a little deeper this time.

"Come out, Noah," yelled Richard. "I just want to talk. Let's work this out."

Sage's spine stiffened as Noah tugged on the rope.

When she's untied, grab Sage and run. I'll distract Richard, Cooper said to Noah.

Noah gave a slight nod showing he agreed with the plan. The fire crackled as Richard made his way back to Sage. Cooper approached him. *You're about to get what's coming to you, you S.O.B.*

"Now," screamed Noah as he jerked Sage back and up.

Richard held up his gun, but Cooper was faster with a kick into the fire that sent flaming logs and ash into Richard's face. Richard screamed in agony as his shirt caught fire. Cooper turned just in time to see Noah and Sage run through the brush towards the trail.

Chapter 36

Slapping out his flaming shirt, Richard fired wildly toward Sage and Noah. His shirt smoldering, he bolted through the woods. Cooper stayed one step ahead of him, snapping back tree limbs, trying to slow Richard's advance. But it was no use. Richard bounced off every defense. Cooper racked his brain trying to think of a way to stop him.

He grabbed another branch and waited for Richard to be in range. As he pulled back, he heard the faint sound of humming. A smile caressed Cooper's face. *I've got you now, pal.*

Cooper eased the branch back to its original spot and found the hole he was looking for. Bees swarmed around the entry, protecting their home. He thrust his hand into the hive, thankful he couldn't be stung. Richard wasn't as lucky. The second he ran by, the bees swarmed him, thinking he was the one who had intruded into their space.

Richard cussed as he tried to swat the swarm away, but they were relentless. Having no luck, he picked up speed and rushed into the dense forest, away from Noah and Sage, trying to lose the bees.

Cooper could hear his screams as he ran away from him. *Ha! That should keep you busy for a while. You should know better than to mess with my girl, you S.O.B.* Cooper focused on Sage, soon finding himself next to her and Noah as they bushwhacked at a steady pace toward Winter Song.

You can use the path now, said Cooper. *Richard will be busy for a while, and he's headed in the opposite direction.*

Noah stopped and grabbed Sage's hand. "Cooper says we can use the trail. We've lost Richard."

"What happened, Cooper? Where is Richard?" asked Sage, and then she shook her head. "I can't believe I'm asking a ghost."

Let's just say, he's getting a bit stung out right now. Cooper proud of himself, laughed loudly at his own joke. *You should've seen it. Those bees were so pissed off at me that they attacked Richard for it. Too bad I didn't think of that while I was trying to keep you away from Sage, huh, Finnley?*

"I think Cooper caused bees to swarm him," said Noah. He looked at Sage's bloody knee. "Are you okay? We should rest. Let me look at that knee."

"I'm fine," said Sage, "besides, we can't stop until we get to Winter Song and call the police. Richard robbed a bank, and he's set on doing worse, Noah. He said he's going to kill you and Lucas. Oh my God, Lexi. Did you find Lexi?"

"We found her. Lucas took her back to Winter Song. He'll take good care of her," said Noah.

"I can't believe he shot her. I would have never thought Richard could be like this, but he almost rape . . . ," she swallowed the rest of the word with a hard gulp. Her voice shaky, she continued. "It's just good you both came around when you did. The look on his face was evil, Noah. Sheer evil." A fresh set of tears started to fall. "I can't image what would've happened if . . ."

Noah pulled her close and hugged her tight. "It's okay. He'll never hurt you again. I won't let anyone hurt you again. I'm sorry I wasn't there for you."

Could we wrap this little love fest up? Those bees are only a distraction. Cooper rolled his eyes. *We need to move.*

"Cooper's right," said Noah. "We need to get going."

Did you just say Cooper's right? The world might just stop moving. Cooper turned around to laugh and saw Richard.

Richard took aim at the couple and fired.

Sage! Cooper shouted desperately, trying to step in front of the bullet. The bullet whooshed right through him. Noah pushed Sage to the ground before falling himself and grasping his thigh.

"Noah!" Sage screamed. "Oh, my God, you're shot!"

Cooper raced by her side. *You have to go, Sage. Run!*

"You have to run. Get out of here." Noah pushed Sage toward the trail. "I'll be fine. Cooper will help me. Now go!"

Cooper looked up at Richard walking slowly up the trail, gun trained on Noah and Sage.

"I can't. He'll kill you," cried Sage. "I love you. I won't leave you."

"I love you, too," Noah brushed her cheek. "That's why you have to go. I couldn't bear it if anything happened to you. Please, run."

Sage shook her head and stood in front of Noah to face Richard. "That's enough, Richard. This ends now."

What are you doing? Cooper groaned. *Get her out of here, Noah.*

Noah looked at Cooper. "You know as well as I do that she won't go now that she's made up her mind. You have to find a way to help her."

Cooper nodded. *I'll do what I can. I left her alone once and promised never to do it again. I won't let her down this time.*

But Cooper knew Noah was right. Sage was a stubborn mule when it came to fighting for those she loved. He moved between Sage and Richard and concentrated on throwing rocks into Richard's face.

"What the . . . ?" Richard's face grew red as he threw his arm up to shield his face from the rocks. He aimed his gun at Sage. Cooper ran toward Richard. Focusing on the gun, he slammed it out of Richard's hand just before he shot. Cooper heard the bullet whizz by his ear and knew it would go left of Sage. He went in for a punch to Richard's gut, but once again his energy was spent. It was all up to Sage now, but at least the gun was no longer a factor.

Staring at his hand in confusion, Richard looked up and then ran at Sage. She planted her feet. *Good girl,* said Cooper. *Now remember what I taught you.*

He came at her full force, but she jumped out of the way just before the tackle. He spun around and was met with her right hook, the same punch she had tried on Cooper just hours before, but this time it met with a solid jaw.

Richard rubbed his jaw. "You're gonna pay for that."

He lunged at Sage, getting her into a headlock. She gasped as he cut her air supply. Cooper spun around looking for something small he might have enough energy to use in order to help Sage, but found nothing.

Noah forced himself up, grabbing Richard from behind and tried to force him off Sage. Using his free hand, Richard reached back and stuck two fingers in Noah's wound, causing Noah to fall to the ground in agony.

Noah's distraction gave Sage just enough time to plant a hard elbow into Richard's diaphragm. She then slammed the back of her fist into his nose. Richard's hold broke as he stumbled backwards trying to catch his breath, blood trickling down his face.

He spat out blood, then gave Sage a wicked smile. "I've changed my mind. I think I *will* kill you. If you love this guy so much, the two of you can spend eternity together in hell."

He sprinted toward Sage. As he went to tackle her, she grabbed his shoulders and stumbled to the ground, kicking him over her body as she rolled onto her back. Gravity did the rest as Richard tumbled over her and sailed through the brush.

Cooper followed Richard, determined to help Sage. She quickly got to her feet and ran to the gun, expecting to see Richard stumble back through the bushes. She froze in place, gun raised at the spot he had fallen. "You'd better run, Richard," she yelled. "I will shoot you."

Cooper came out from the brush. *Tell Sage its okay*, he said to Noah. *Richard's not coming. She can put the gun down.*

"Cooper says its okay," Noah said gently to Sage. "You can put the gun down."

"He'll kill us all!" yelled Sage, panic engulfing her face. "We need to stop him. He won't be satisfied until we're all dead."

Cooper appeared by Sage's side and brushed her hair. Her eyes fell shut as she felt Cooper's signature move and released a deep breath. *Its okay, baby. Richard won't be back. I'll deal with the bastard now. You've done everything you could. Now it's my turn.*

Noah reached up and eased the gun out of Sage's trembling hand.

"Sage, you can put the gun down." Noah dropped his head. "Richard's dead."

Chapter 37

"Dead?" Sage covered her mouth with her hand as tears pooled in her eyes. "How?"

Noah looked at Cooper, who was watching the brush intently. "You heard her, Cooper, answer the question."

He was impaled by a tree. Looks like the tree was hit by lightning in the last storm. He fell on it and never knew what hit him. Cooper cracked his knuckles. Noah relayed the message to Sage as she bent to apply pressure to his wound with her still trembling hands.

But he will, Cooper continued. *As soon as his spirit comes out of his body, he's in for the beating of his life, or should I say after-life.* He smiled. *He should've never hurt Sage, but I'll make him pay. I've been waiting all night for this.*

"He's not coming," Noah said, shaking his head at Cooper. "You won't see him."

What do you mean? asked Cooper. *I've been waiting for this.*

"Who's not coming? What's going on?" Sage looked at Noah.

"Richard's spirit. Cooper wants to punch his face in on a spiritual plane, but it doesn't work that way." Noah bowed his head. "Richard never had a light, so he never had a choice. Only those who die a good death, get the choice about whether to move on or stay behind and check on loved ones. He's answering to a higher power now."

Are you kidding me? Cooper threw punches in the air. *That's a load of crap.*

Noah looked up at Cooper. "Just be glad you died a good death."

Sage glanced at the sky, swallowing the scream of grief that threatened to escape. "May God have mercy on his soul. He was a good friend to me for a long time. I'm just sorry it all ended this way." She looked back at Noah. "We need to get you back to Winter Song. Can you walk?"

Noah grimaced as he stood. "I think it's just a flesh wound. It would be bleeding more had he hit an artery." He glanced at Cooper. "Hate to tell you this, but I'll live."

Cooper rolled his eyes. *Good thing, I believe we have a fight to finish once my energy gets back up.*

Noah shook his head. "I'm done fighting with you, Cooper. It's up to Sage now. If she wants you here then I'll relay your important messages before leaving. But if she wants you gone, you need to go into the light and respect her wishes."

Sage's eyes begged Noah not to make her choose. "I can't . . ."

"Don't worry," said Noah, "you've got time to think about it. You don't have to decide right now. I'll wait 'till you're okay with your answer. It doesn't matter how long it takes. But I won't play walkie-talkie with you and Cooper. I just can't do that."

"I understand," said Sage. "It's just that I've loved Coop for a long time, and I love you now. I want you both, but I know that's not fair."

She doesn't have to decide at all, said Cooper. *I made a promise out there that I intend to keep. I'm going into the light, but don't tell her just yet. Let's give her some time to digest everything that's happened. I don't want to lay more bad news on her right this moment.*

Noah leaned on Sage as they hobbled down the trail. Less than an hour later, they were met by Lucas, EMTs, and police officers. Sage explained to the officers where they could find Richard's body, and they hurried down the path. The EMTs confirmed Noah's wound was not serious. "It looks like it went clean through, but we'll know more once we get you to the hospital," one of the EMTs explained. "The men with the stretcher will be here shortly. Until then, don't move. I'm going on ahead, to see if I can help."

Sage looked at Lucas. "Lexi?"

Lucas shook his head sadly. "I'm sorry to tell you this, Sage, but she didn't make it. The bullet wound was too severe. She was in my arms when she passed. She did not die alone."

Sage bowed her head as fresh tears started to fall. "She was a good dog. I can't believe she's gone."

That bastard Richard better be glad he doesn't have to answer to me. I can't believe he killed her. If I ever see him again, he's gonna wish he . . . Cooper trailed off.

"That's not going to happen, Cooper, things are different there. The way I understand it, you just kind of lose that anger," said Noah, getting a sympathetic look from Sage and Lucas.

"Where is he?" Sage asked Noah. "I want to talk to him. Will you help me?"

Noah nodded and then pointed to his right. She sighed as she turned to face where Cooper stood, her tears even more abundant. "Coop, I love you. I always will. The love you and I had will never leave my heart. But it's time for you to go. I love you even more for coming back to me, and for protecting me. But now it's my turn . . . my turn to protect you from yourself. It's time for you to go into the light."

I know I said I was going, but . . . Cooper gave her a sad smile. *I said I'd never leave you again, and I meant it. You need me. Tonight is proof of that. I just can't help but think I'm breaking my promise to you by going into the light. But I want you to be happy.*

"He said he feels like he's breaking his promise to never leave you alone again," Noah said. "He wants you to be happy and to make sure nothing like tonight ever happens again."

"But I'm not alone, Coop." Sage looked around her. "I have Noah and your dad. You need to go to the light. You need to be at peace. Knowing you're not staying around watching me live the life we planned together, will make me happy. Please go into the light. It's time for you to go on to the next adventure. It's time for you to be reunited with your mom."

I promised God that if he helped me get you out of this mess . . . if he got you out of this safe and sound, that I would go to the light. And I will keep that promise because you've asked me to and because He helped me when I most needed it.

"Cooper promised God that if He helped get you through tonight unhurt, he would go into the light. He's keeping that promise to God and honoring your wishes. He's very thankful you're safe," said Noah.

Lucas stepped forward. "Son, I am so sorry for what I did to you and your mother." His voice cracked. "Please, tell her she is my soul mate, and I will see her again. We will live another life together, one of happiness."

He cleared his throat, stood tall, and continued. "Until then, I will stay here at Winter Song and do my best to make amends for all the wrong I have done in this lifetime by helping and protecting Sage as best I can. It is where I am meant to be now. I cannot ask you to forgive me, but it is my hope one day we will meet again, and you will have found it in your heart to do so."

Cooper stared into his father's watery eyes. *Its okay, Dad. I already have.*

He placed his hand on Lucas's shoulder. Lucas looked at Noah, who gave him a quick nod confirming what he felt was his son. "Thank you, Son." Wiping his eyes, Lucas turned toward Winter Song. "I will go now and give you all some privacy."

Cooper watched his dad disappear down the trail before looking at Sage. *If only I would've listened to you and not gotten on that stupid boat, things would be so different.* He kicked the ground in frustration. *I don't want to tell you good-bye. You were always the best part of me. I can't imagine not being with you every day as I have for over a year. I will miss you more than you will ever know. I will always love you, and I'll be watching from wherever I'm going now.* He rubbed his eyes, surprised to find tears. *I would give the world to hold you one last time.*

He stared at Noah and pointed at Sage. *You tell her everything I've said just now. Leave nothing out. That's the least you can do for me, Finnley. Go ahead and make the light.*

Noah nodded and concentrated on an old tall pine tree. A lighted doorway appeared, and Cooper walked toward it. As he approached, Lexi came running out of the bushes. She jumped into Cooper's arms and licked his face. Cooper could feel her soft fur as he scratched her head. *Devil dog, I'm glad you're here.*

Noah smiled, then whispered to Sage, "Lexi is with Cooper. They are going into the light together."

Sage let out a loud sob, but smiled. "I'm glad they have each other."

Cooper looked over his shoulder at Noah as he and Lexi walked into the light. *She's too good for us.*

"I know," said Noah.

Chapter 38

Six Months Later

Sage rubbed the head of the brown and white fluff ball. The little puppy barked playfully before rolling over onto her back, big ears flopping open. Sage giggled and rubbed the puppy's round belly.

"You're too much," Sage said to the puppy, picking it up and snuggling it close. "I can't believe anyone would leave you little guys out by the highway."

"They will be good dogs," said Lucas, sitting beside Sage. "I've already found homes for five of them. The runt," he pointed to the puppy in Sage's arms, "will stay with us if you don't mind. I thought we could name her Tilly. It means mighty in battle. She can sleep out here with me."

"I think that's a great idea," said Sage. "The barn is yours to do with as you please. Besides, I've missed having a dog here at Winter Song."

Sage stood and headed toward the door. "I've got to go. Noah needs some help with the new dock."

"Do you still miss Cooper?" asked Lucas.

Sage stopped. "Every day, but not in the way you'd imagine. I miss his laugh and his corny jokes. I miss being able to talk to him. But the pain lessens a bit as time goes on, and I'm happy with Noah . . . so happy. I know that's what Coop wanted when he left. Noah never needed to relay that message. Coop had his flaws, but he always wanted me to be happy."

"Yes, I believe his soul is at peace." Lucas shook his head. "Go now, Noah is waiting."

As Sage moseyed toward the lake, she noticed something floating in the water. Squinting her eyes she could make out flashes of red, purple, white, pink and blue, but she couldn't really tell what the objects were. She looked up to see Noah standing on the end of the newly built dock overlooking the lake. He looked breathtaking in his khaki pants and untucked white button up shirt. Sage couldn't help but smile as she got closer and realized the objects in the lake were flower petals.

"Somebody is feeling romantic," she teased.

Noah took her hand and planted a deep kiss on her. Then lowering to one knee, he reached for something in his pocket.

Sage gasped as Noah opened a black felt box containing a pear-shaped diamond engagement ring.

Acknowledgments

Wow, I am so very blessed. I have so many people in my life who shared their love and support with me and made this book possible.

First, I'd like to thank the staff at LilyBear House. You guys are the best, I couldn't do it without y'all. Diana Purser, I appreciate all your hard work on copy edits, thanks for being the guru. A special thank you to Cheryl Trenfield, Christina Laurie, and Bill Johnson for your final edits, I appreciate your eagle eyes more than I can say. Brandy Walker from Sister Sparrow Graphic Design, you are beyond talented and I feel so privileged to have your cover art on my books. Thank you for all your hard work.

I would be remiss if I didn't thank Marilyn Boone, Heather Davis and Denise Jarmola, I could not have done this without you gals. Thanks for finding the holes and working with me to smooth out the rough edges. To the WordWeavers, you guys are the best. Thanks for keeping me motivated, your support means the world to me. To Claressa Carter and Rubina Ahmed, a girl is lost without besties, thanks for being mine. To Darlene Shortridge and Linda Boulanger, a girl couldn't ask for better mentors and friends. Thanks for always being around to answer my questions.

To my family, each and every one of you, from aunts to uncles to grandparents to cousins to in-laws. I love you all, and I am who I am today because of the influence each and every one of you have on me.

Thanks for being awesome. To my mother, Cathy Collar, I'm so glad we're on this journey together. I am so proud of you. Your skills as a writer, have made me improve mine. I am in awe of your imagination and flair for all things fantasy. To my father, Randy Collar, I owe my strong work ethic and drive to you. Thanks for never letting me take the easy way out. And to my special angel in heaven, Anna. I miss you every day.

To my ever supportive and loving husband, Mike. Thank you for reading every word, even when you had a million other things to do. It is because of you that I'm not only following my dream, but living it. I love you more than words can say. I am so very blessed to have you. Oh and one more thing . . . BINGO!

And finally, to my dear sweet baby girl. I am so very blessed to have you. Your smile lights my world and with every hug, I just want to try harder, for you. You are by far the best kid. You are my joy. You are my everything. I love you, Bug.

If you enjoyed *Winter Song*,
Summer's End is now available where fine
books are sold

Also by
Jennifer McMurrain

Summer's End

Enjoy an Excerpt from
Summer's End

"You can't surf in that." Tyler pointed at Jessica's skimpy bikini before gesturing to the North Carolina waves coming on shore. "It'll come off with the first wipeout."

"Thought you'd prefer it that way." Jessica laughed, winking at him. "Besides, you know very well I don't surf. I tan."

Tyler ran his hand along his red and yellow surfboard. "Well, since this is our last day together I thought you might like to give it a try. You'll regret it if you don't."

Jessica threw her arms around his neck. "And I thought since this was our last day together, you'd skip the surfing and cuddle with me on the beach."

"Seems we're at an impasse." Tyler gave her a sexy smirk before dropping the board and wrapping his arms around her waist. He kissed her. "I guess I could surf tomorrow after you've gone back to Oklahoma."

She cringed and pushed him away. "We promised never to say the *O word*."

Tyler playfully grabbed her hand and pulled her back into his arms. "You know you don't have to go."

"You know I do." Jessica sighed as she laid her head on his broad chest. "I have to finish my degree. I only have one semester left and it would be stupid for me not to finish at Oklahoma State. Just think, in six months I can come back here, get a job, and stick to you like glue until you're sick of me."

Tyler's silence prompted Jessica to squeeze him tightly. "You know I don't want to go. If I could, I'd stay right here in your arms forever. I love you, Tyler."

"I love you, too," said Tyler, giving her a kiss on the top of her head.

"Let's not talk about this, baby," said Jessica, looking up into Tyler's mocha colored eyes. "Let's make a deal. You forget about me going back to ... well, you know where ... and I'll try to surf."

He met her gaze, forehead wrinkled. "Really, you'll try?"

Jessica eyed the board. "I don't see the appeal, but you're right. I'll regret it if I don't at least try."

He turned and kissed her hard. "You're going to love it. I promise."

After more than a few failed attempts and wicked wipeouts, Tyler conceded that Jessica was not a surfer. The couple spent the rest of the day swimming and kissing within the waves. As the sun drifted down into a beautiful Carolina sunset, Jessica paddled to catch one last wave and attempt to surf. She wanted to prove to Tyler that she could do it. Tyler cheered her on as she reached the crest and attempted to pop up. The wave crashed into her and everything went black, followed by a blinding white light.

"Jessica. Jessica, wake up."

Jessica felt a hand shaking her shoulder and reached up to grab it. "Tyler?"

The hand jerked away. "It's your mother. It's three o'clock in the afternoon, and you've been sleeping all day. I thought you were going to look for a job today."

Jessica sat up and looked around the room. She was in her parents' house. She flopped back down.

"You can't live like this, Jessica. It's not healthy and it's not right." Her mother walked around Jessica's room picking up dirty laundry. "This room is filthy and you sleep all the time. I can't even imagine why or how someone would want to sleep her life away."

Jessica stared out the window, taking in the horizon of grass in the field outside her window blowing in the wind like ocean waves. Wiping a tear from her eye, she whispered. "Because that's the only place where I can see him."

Her mother sighed heavily as she dropped the dirty laundry in the hamper. "Jessica, honey, it's been two years. It's time to move on. Now get up and take a shower. You stink."

"Thanks a lot, Myra," Jessica muttered.

"And don't call me Myra. I don't care how old you are, I am your mother. You will call me Mom," Myra snapped as she walked out of Jessica's bedroom.

Jessica waited for her mother to close the door before exiting the bed. She shuffled to the desk at the far side of the room and took a small shoebox out of the bottom drawer. Inside were all her mementos from her summer interning in North Carolina.

She smiled at each memory, tracing the faces in the photos of her first day at the dig site with the other college interns. At last she came to the bottom of the box where a single newspaper clipping lay open. Tyler's obituary, dated two days after she returned to Oklahoma.

Returning the items into the box, she grabbed her stuffed rabbit and went back to her bed. She desperately wanted to return to her dream with Tyler. She closed her eyes and listened in her head to the rhythmic ocean waves washing over the shore. Soon she was back at the beach where Tyler stood scanning the water, panic written all over his face.

"Tyler," said Jessica, running to him. She was again in her bikini, the grass fields a distant memory.

Tyler ran to her and wrapped her in a tight hug. "That was quite some wipe out. Are you okay?"

"I'm fine," said Jessica, realizing she was wet.

Tyler picked up a towel off the sand and wrapped it around her shoulders. "How 'bout we call it a day. We'll have some dinner, and then I'll help you pack."

"I've changed my mind," said Jessica, smiling. "I've decided to stay in North Carolina."

"Really?" Tyler beamed. "You mean it? What about college?"

"I don't need it," said Jessica. "I'll get a job as a maid at one of the hotels if I have to. I just don't want to leave you again."

"Are you sure, Jessica?" asked Tyler, his smile fading. "This is a big move. What about your degree? You've worked so hard and you only have a semester left. Your parents will be beyond upset."

"They'll get over it," said Jessica with a shrug. "I'm an adult now and I get to make my own decisions. I don't care about my degree anymore. I only care about you."

"I don't know," said Tyler, shaking his head.

"You don't want me here?" asked Jessica.

"You know I do," said Tyler, "more than anything. But I don't want you to throw your whole life away because of me. I don't want you to change your plans and not get your degree. That makes me feel like I'm being selfish."

Jessica gave him a little peck on the nose. "I love you even more because of how unselfish you're being right now, but my mind is made up. I'm staying. The rest we'll figure out as we go."

"Jessica!"

"Who's that?" asked Tyler, looking around for the person who had just screamed Jessica's name.

"No one," answered Jessica, knowing full well it was her mother. "Just ignore her."

"Jessica Lyn Collins, you get up right this minute!" yelled Myra.

"I better go," said Tyler.

"No," cried Jessica, "don't go."

Before she could hold him there, Jessica's mom dumped a cup of cold water over her.

"Mom!" Jessica screamed, stunned from the cold water. "What's the matter with you?"

"What's the matter with me?" Myra slammed the plastic Eskimo Joe's cup down on the bedside table. "What's the matter with you? I told you to get up and take a shower. I don't know how you can possibly go back to sleep after sleeping all day. This isn't right, Jessica. I'm taking you to Dr. Upton tomorrow and that's final."

"I don't need to see Dr. Upton," said Jessica, wiping her face with her sheet. "I'm fine."

"There is nothing fine about what you're doing." Myra sighed. "This is my fault. I should've taken you to see Dr. Upton a while ago. Grief is hard, and I guess I didn't think this fling was that serious."

"It wasn't a fling, Mom," retorted Jessica.

"You weren't there long enough for anything else," said Myra.

"I loved him, Mom," said Jessica, picking at the embroidered flowers on her bedspread, hoping she wouldn't cry again.

Myra sat on the bed next to Jessica and gently laid her hand on Jessica's shoulder. "I believe you, and that's why we're going to go see Dr. Upton. He can give you some medicine to help with your grief and to help get your sleep cycle back under control. What you're doing now, hon, it just isn't healthy. Maybe he can recommend someone for you to talk to." Myra gave Jessica a little hug. "Now seriously, get up and take a shower before your father gets home. You really do stink."

About the Author

Having a great deal of wanderlust, Author Jennifer McMurrain traveled the countryside working odd jobs before giving into her muse and becoming a full time writer. She's been everything from a "Potty Princess" in the wilds of Yellowstone National Park to a Bear Researcher in the mountains of New Mexico. After finally settling down, she received a Bachelor's degree in Applied Arts and Science from Midwestern State University in Wichita Falls, TX. She has won numerous awards for her short stories and novels. She lives in Bartlesville, Oklahoma with her husband, daughter, two spoiled cats, and two goofy dogs. Winter Song is her second novel.

Author photograph by Brandy Walker Photography

Novels

Quail Crossings
Return to Quail Crossings
Missing Quail Crossings
Summer's End

Novellas

The Looking Glass
The Divine Heart
Birdsong
Heart of an Angel

Collaborations & Anthologies

A Weekend with Effie
Seasons of Life
Seasons Remembered
Chicken Soup for the Soul: The Dog Did What?
Amore: A Mini Romantic Anthology
Whispered Beginnings

Short Stories

Thesis Revised
Emma's Walk
Footprints in the Snow
Finding Hope
Jar of Pickles

Friend Author Jennifer McMurrain on Facebook:
https://www.facebook.com/pages/Author-Jennifer-
McMurrain

Follow Jennifer's tweets -
https://twitter.com/Deepbluejc

Visit her on her website:
http://www.jennifermcmurrain.com